Christ, Myself and the Young People

Reaching out to Young People
with the Good News of Salvation

G000162468

Joy Sebastian

2016

Christ, Myself and the Young People — published by the Rev. Dr. Ashish Amos of the Indian Society for Promoting Christian Knowledge (ISPCK), Post Box 1585, Kashmere Gate, Delhi-110006.

© Author, 2016

All rights reserved. No part of this book may be reproduced or transmitted in any form or by any means, electronic, mechanical, photocopying, recording, or by any information storage and retrieval system, without the prior permission in writing from the publisher.

The views expressed in the book are those of the author and the publisher takes no responsibility for any of the statements.

Online order: http://ispck.org.in/book.php

Also available on amazon.in

ISBN: 978-81-8465-553-7

e-book ISBN: 978-81-8465-554-4

Laser typeset by

ISPCK, Post Box 1585, 1654, Madarsa Road, Kashmere Gate, Delhi-110006 • *Tel:* 23866323

e-mail: ashish@ispck.org.in • ella@ispck.org.in
website: www.ispck.org.in

Dedicated

to

Anastasia Lepcha,

Rudyard William

and

Reginald William

Contents

Part - 1
A Personal Odyssey

Part - 2
A Spiritual Journey

Acknowledgements

I would like to express my deep gratitude to Rev. Dipankar Nath of the Methodist Church in India for writing the preface and for making me aware of my vocation. Rev. Fr. (Dr). Shinoj K TOR, the Principal of St. Francis School, and the parish priest who has encouraged me constantly to continue with my preaching and writing. My association with this beautiful mind is providence. I am also grateful to Rev. Fr. Joe Brennan SJ, the most gifted spiritual counsellor and a remarkable Jesuit formator; for his spiritual guidance, patience and his critical estimation of my work. I will never forget the cooperation, advice and assistance of Rev. Fr. Alvin Minj SJ and Rev. Fr. Pramode Dhabi SJ, the Director of *Jesu Ashram* during my stay there. My grateful thanks is also extended to Mr. Robi Subba, the Director of Himali Boarding School, Kurseong, for allowing me to interact with the students of class XI and XII and for his help during my stay in Kurseong. Mr. Subba is a man of remarkable hospitality. The former Principal of Mount Hermon School, Darjeeling, Mr. Terrence Wharton has also encouraged me after reading my first book 'Amazing Grace'. I am indebted to his generosity.

I would also like to extend my thanks to the General Secretary, Rev. Dr. Ashish Amos, ISPCK.

Finally, I wish to thank my parents for their prayers and support.

My former students and colleagues of Himali Boarding School, Kurseong are always in my prayers. God bless this edifice of learning!

And a very special thanks to my dear friend Fr. Shiju Mathew, S.J. (Administrations, Indian Social Institute, New Delhi) for his genuine support.

Preface

I seize this opportunity to write the preface for the Book entitled "Christ, Myself and the Young People" written by my beloved friend Rev. Sebastian Joy, who is a renowned teacher, preacher and a blessing from God to us. This book itself explains the experience of the writer, and how he has used the opportunity to share the good news of our master Jesus Christ to young people.

All over the world, the present young generation is after their career and worldly lust, where we as Christians need to remember that we are a chosen generation with a purpose for His glory. The ultimate authority in this universe clearly declares that we should remember Him at our young age (Ecclesiastes 12:1). But how can a young man or woman receive the good news unless we tell them. As parents we often encourage them to build their career and believe that they should get involved in spiritual affairs after they get settled in their life. It is absolutely wrong because God has clearly revealed His desire for us to give our prime time to Him for His glory.

I am thankful to the author who has dedicated his life for God and His ministry. The author has expressed his practical experiences and desire for work among the young generation which is highly appreciated. Let me remind ourselves that we are not responsible or accountable for the past or future generation but our own generation which God has entrusted on us.

I give thanks to Rev. Sebastian who took the initiative to write for the young generation what God has laid in his heart. I wish and pray for his success as he is pursuing the purpose God has set before him. I have faith in God that reading this book will give readers a new dimension of faith and instill a desire to do more for our young generation. May God bless each one of us. In Him

Rev. Dipankar Nath
Elder, Methodist Church in India,
Bengal Regional Conference.
Dated: 22nd April, 2016.

Introduction

reetings in the name of our Lord and Saviour Jesus Christ!

It was a cold and quite evening. The end of October was happily felt all around, in the distant valleys and among the flowers. I could see through my window sills the infinite azure skies and the stunning mountain ranges. It was definitely a moment of great joy! I asked my cook to make some tea for us and was elated with the idea of reading some good poetry. No sooner did I open Palgrave's *Golden Treasury* than I heard a knock at my door. It was 6 pm by my watch and at that time of the year it was unusual for some visitor to call on a young preacher at his residence. The door of my room was opened and to my surprise I discovered a young girl from a nearby school standing with a hesitant gesture. She was not a stranger as she used to see me often and shared her grieves and agonies. However, I was little surprised by seeing her and without wasting much time, I accompanied her into my parlour. She was comfortably seated and I asked Sonam, my cook and companion to provide the girl with some warm soup. She refused the offer and began to sob, rather I found her panting. As a psychoanalyst, I was taught to keep quite when the other person cries or talks about his or her problems. I have always been an obedient pupil and never tried anything different. (Though of late, I find a growing tendency among counselors to talk a lot and give advises when they are supposed to keep quite.)

The evening passed, I had lost another precious day from my life. The young girl who visited me last evening and had stayed for almost an hour, left my home happily. I did not have a good sleep that night. Something was constantly pricking me in my mind. A strong sense of unfulfillment. The next morning I consoled myself saying that it was a plain tale of love and lovelessness, of affairs and their merciless ends…very common among the youth, especially those are in their adolescence. From class 9 onwards…

In between, nothing unusual happened. After a week or two I was called by the principal of a renowned school to attend a funeral service in a place 20 kms away from my place. To my surprise I had learnt that I was accompanying a group of 45 students along with their principal to attend the funeral of the girl who had visited me only a fortnight before! My episode with that particular girl ended in a small Christian graveyard almost 5500 feet above the sea level. But that very incident marked the beginning of the most decisive journey of my life. And that is treading the apparently difficult and inaccessible path holding the hand of my Lord and Saviour Jesus Christ. Be it a session of counseling or taking a class, without Christ everything is incomplete and every endeavour is futile. I had learnt a few psychological terms, a few methods of psycho analysis; I have developed my own methodology: but what was missing was the GRACE, the AMAZING GRACE! I have no objection to the modern secular counseling, but what I have felt is something much more deep and sublime. It is all about having Christ with you every time, every moment or having nothing with you at all.

Thus, I have decided to write down my experiences from that time onwards with the youth. I have been travelling, teaching and preaching in the Himalayan foothill region of Darjeeling. The name Darjeeling readily brings to our mind the most charming hill station with the magnanimous Mount Kanchendzongha! Its rich variety of flora and fauna: and of course the world famous Darjeeling Tea. But it is also famous for having old, famous and prestigious schools in all its three subdivisions (Darjeeling, Kurseong and Kalimpong). A few remarkable ones are St. Paul's, St. Joseph, Mount Hermon, St. Helen, Himali Boarding School, Dr. Graham's Homes etc. These schools not only provide the students with quality education, but also make the students competent and smart enough to adjust with any kind of environment. But in this world of consumerism, a child can hardly stay away from all sorts of material allurements. Virtual needs are gaining prominence over the real needs. In some cases, the parents are even providing their wards with expensive items and gadgets. Sports gear of foreing brands are becoming basic requirements. Children, whose parents find it difficult to afford foreign brands, borrow money to meet their children's demands.

In such cases we cannot blame the parents either. The schools try to impart enough moral and spiritual lessons to the children, but exposure to the nearest shopping mall or to television makes things different. Not necessarily a physician to cure them of cough or migraine, but a doctor to cure the torments of their soul. A true Doctor of Soul can really make things different. In most cases, schools run by Christian missionaries follow psycho-spiritual counseling which is the best method to heal a troubled soul. Many schools appoint secular counsellors or psychologists to motivate their children. There is no conflict between the two, but in the long run psycho spiritual counseling helps the soul to convert, thus saving a child from catastrophe. I have experienced that pastors, religious brothers and sisters, priests are the best counselors. Whatever they do, they do as a part of their ministry. They do not expect any material benefit in return. I am very happy to have a long and steady relationship with such spiritual counsellors. In this connection I must mention the name of Fr. Joe Brennan SJ. He is probably the best man we have ever had

I have deliberately and thoughtfully changed the real names of the students and the schools to which they belonged. Many of them are in touch with me. However, the problems faced by the students at their early stage gradually disappeared as soon as they realized the presence of Lord Jesus Christ into their life. So problems and difficulties have become insignificant. Similarly, my emphasis is not on the negative aspect of their lives, but on the positive, i.e. how I have succeeded in making them aware of the everlasting love of Jesus Christ and how the Lord himself has helped them to find a permanent solution to their problems. It is all about the troubled youth and the kind of relationship they have with Jesus.

Therefore, let us recall what Jesus had answered to the Devil while the former was tempted:

> One doesnot live on bread alone, but on every word that comes from the mouth of God. (Matthew 4:4)

We do not live by bread alone. And the words of God are written down in the Holy Bible. So, according to Christ, if the words of God are taken away from us then we will not only starve, but we will cease to live. And it is what is happening all around. Many of us have o conscious, no compassion, no zeal to live for others. Just to live life to the fullest, to enjoy life to the fullest, and to care for nothing. When the virtual image overshadows the real image, the self degenerates, it dies. Why shall we die before our time comes? Is not life precious? God has made us in His own image and Christ has paid a ransom for all of us dying on the cross.

I consider that our present sufferings are not worth comparing with the glory that will be revealed in us. For the creation waits in eager expectation for the children of God to be revealed. For the creation was subjected to frustration, not by its own choice, but by the will of the one who subjected it, in hope that the creation itself will be liberated from its bondage to decay and brought into the freedom and glory of the children of God. **(Romans 8: 18-21)**

"We do, however, speak a message of wisdom among the mature, but not the wisdom of this age or of the rulers of this age, who are coming to nothing. No, we declare God's wisdom, a mystery that has been hidden and that God destined for our glory before time began. None of the rulers of this age understood it, for if they had, they would not have crucified the Lord of glory. However, as it is written:

What no eye has seen,

what no ear has heard,

and what no human mind has conceived"

the things God has prepared for those who love him—

these are the things God has revealed to us by his Spirit.

(1 Corinth 2: 6-10)

In His service,

Joy Sebastian

Shamli, April 23rd

Part – 1
A Personal Odyssey

1

Spring 2010, St. Mary's Hills

It was a class of twenty-four small children enjoying their school life in one of the reputed boarding schools. The students were innocent and each of them had a story to tell every evening after supper. Generally, in boarding schools students go for a second round prep class after supper. The time to go to bed is usually 9 pm. I was staying in the premise of the school and had to interact with a number of students. The timing allotted to me by the Principal was the hours between four and six. In the beginning I hardly had any student to see me in my chamber. But as days passed and the tedious monsoon had set in, I found the level of depression gradually increased among the students. In the hills we get ceaseless rain for days and weeks. At times it becomes really frustrating. You don't have much work to do and at the same time you cannot even walk into the town. Climbing downhill becomes increasingly difficult when it pours and the chances of getting a vehicle become remote.

Boarders usually play in the school ground in the evening and when it rains, they are kept inside. At that time the desire to see a pastor or a spiritual guide reaches its zenith. With or without reason students are found gathering around the chapel. Most of them are people of other faith and they literally enjoy Bible classes in their schools. You might find a Christian boy or girl running away from the Bible class but the students of other faith are ever ready with their copies of the New Testament. There is a beautiful secular environment inside the boarding schools of Darjeeling, Kurseong and Kalimpong. I don't know what happens when these kids grow up!

During such a solitary monsoon day, I happened to meet Sucheta, Juliana, Poonam and Sobina. They were in their eighth standard and Sobina was from one of our neighbouring countries. In the residential schools of the hills you find a number of students from Bangladesh, Bhutan, Nepal, Myanmar, Thailand and Singapore, though the number has begun to decrease. Sobina was not only shy but she looked very scared. She assumed the role of the leader when they had come to see me for the first time. I was under the impression that they were afraid of their text books so they were in need of my prayer and counseling. However the thing which was revealed was something of a peculiar manner. It was much connected to a third rate Bollywood horror movie.

They used to see ghosts; at times the ghosts sat beside them on the bed without making any noise. Children staying away from their parents suffer from various psychological disorders. They may not be serious but one should not ignore them. It is always good for the counselor to listen carefully to what the children disclose. I too allowed those girls to speak out their mind spontaneously. Juliana was talkative and very intelligent. She knew all the ways to stay away from the evening preps; either by hiding inside the washroom or by sitting quietly inside the infirmary. But she failed to chase the ghosts away from her room. After listening to their stories for many days I was convinced that they have mild anxiety disorder; as their class teacher already told me. It could be because of their home sickness. Obsessive-compulsive disorder is commonly found among the hostel students. I thought of sending them to the school counselor but their Principal dissuaded me from so doing. Then I secretly developed a methodology to deal with their 'Ghost-Disorder'.

It was a holiday in the month of September. Things around started changing. The incessant rains had gently subsided and the children had occasions again to play in the green fields. The girls came to me with some other story but I changed the topic and asked them about the colours on the wall and of those ghosts at night. I was certain about one thing that all of them were afraid of ghosts and the problem was not complex psychological disorder, but a fear somewhere in the depth of their hearts. "Yes Sir, we still feel some one present in the dormitory and particularly when we get up in the night to go to the washroom, someone follows us...", the same old tale of gothic horror and romance. I asked them whether they know about the master of the ghosts. They looked surprised and answered me 'No'. I was expecting the same answer and I told them that there is only one master of the ghosts and that was Jesus. They were shocked and dumbfounded. They never expected such a thing from a preacher. I insisted and made them belief that if they pray to Jesus then the ghosts would run away. I don't think any one of them believed me, but they had no other way. They had tried all possible and impossible means. Before it was time for their evening prep, I had taught them a simple prayer, and had written that prayer on a piece of paper from my pad. It was:

Lord Jesus, we believe in you

and we love you very much,

You know that ghosts come to disturb us every night

And we are very much scared.

Please drive them away as you have done so many times.

In your name the apostles had driven away demons

And if you don't help us

Then we have no other hope.

You died for us

You love us,

And please tell the ghosts to go away from our dormitory.

Amen.

It might appear funny to some pastors, priests or theologians but I was convinced that Lord Jesus would surely help those girls. I told them not to make the sign of the cross (and to stay away from other non-biblical rituals as there was a teacher influencing the students with all these stuff) and not to say any prayer except the Lord's Prayer which they knew very well.

They prayed religiously, and every night before going to bed they prayed. The warden once told me that four girls from class eight regularly prayed a very 'funny' prayer. In a week or two their friends too joined them. Then it became a matter of discussion in the parlour that the entire girls' dormitory prays together before going to bed. The most surprising news was that, the warden and his wife began to enjoy the blessing of God in form of good sleep. And how was that?

Brother, you won't believe that the girls don't even call me now at night, even when they go to the bathroom!

Said Kalpana, the warden's wife.

I tried and Jesus did the rest for me. I had succeeded in bringing Jesus among a few school children coming from absolutely no Christian background, and I know that they had felt the love of our Lord and His gentle touch. Besides, I was informed that those girls surprisingly changed their attitude and habits and had become decent and diligent. The day I was transferred to another school, I had gifted each of them with a Bible and a notebook. I remember the date, it was the 5th of September.

The notebook was given to write down their experiences of personal encounter with Jesus. I am sure they are now in colleges or universities. Some of them might have got married. They will, in some way or the other, definitely share with their friends, children or relatives how Lord Jesus helped them once in their life.

2

The Intolerable

He was intolerable not because I had a pejorative feeling towards him; on the contrary I began to like him from the third day of his arrival. He was angry with everything and was moody and idiosyncratic. He came from Kolkata but had no resemblance of a Calcutta boy. Rather he was like a misfit trying to adjust with the most impossible environment in a boarding school almost 5000 feet above the sea level. It became evident to me that he had either failed his class 11 final examinations in his former school or he was rusticated for his conduct. To my understanding, both these unfortunate events occurred to him simultaneously.

It was the middle of the session when he took admission and to my surprise I found him dozing in the last bench when I was teaching the 'murder scene' of Shakespeare's *Macbeth*. In those days, we taught Macbeth in class 11. Reading Shakespeare was like torture to him and he candidly admitted the very fact that to him studying was something abominable. There was nothing unusual about his reflections on studies but what was unusual was his wild temperament. He was untamed and rude.

At times he was violent. There were frequent complaints as to his conducts both in the dormitory and in the refectory. The warden was exhausted after having experienced him only for a week. The Principal, one of the most refined gentlemen, looked miserably pale and helpless after having a session of counseling with him.

The only possibility of keeping him in the hostel was to take him to a good psychiatrist and get him the help he needed. Things happened as per the plans of the Principal and one fine morning he was accompanied by his House Master to the best psychiatrist in the town. People were happy, his parents were indifferent and the boy was glad as he had a grand outing and a sumptuous supper. I felt relaxed after a long time as he was creating a lot of nuisances in the classrooms. He was under medication and things went well for quite some time until one evening I heard a terrible noise from the boys' dormitory. No sooner did we rush into the dormitory than he fled breaking a couple of tube lights and destroying the porcelain statue of the patron saint of the School. I did not mind his breaking the idol but he was no Martin Luther. He was not assaulted or punished. The Principal was hurt and he ordered his secretary to call up the boy's parents and to prepare a transfer certificate in no time.

That evening I walked into his dormitory and sat beside him. He was lying down and did not bother to get up and wish me. I wanted to make him comfortable and my intention was to share a few words with him in a casual friendly manner. I wished him good evening but it was not answered. I went on asking him about his hobbies and favourite games. It took me almost half an hour to convince him that I was not his adversary but his friend and was willing to help him out from all the troubles and tensions that he was carrying on his shoulder. At last he began to hum a popular tune, I insisted him to go ahead and after a few minutes he started singing aloud.

"Sir, can you sing?"

"Well, if situation demands I can try." was my humble reply.

"Sing me a song" he added.

I hesitated and was literally struggling to choose an easy hymn when suddenly he exclaimed: "What a great tune *Emptyness* has!"

The song he referred to was once very popular in the hills and it had attracted many immature hearts craving for love.

That night, after having my supper I went to see my friend in the sanatorium. There we had a long discussion on the problems of children especially in the boarding schools. I sought his advice regarding the troublemaker whom I was dealing with. My friend had suggested me to send him to a good counselor and get him treated. Somehow his suggestion did not appeal to me because the boy had already visited a renowned psychiatrist but so far no development came to our notice. In a way we all gave up. Besides, the boy was about to go home in a day or two. I returned from my friend's place late and asked my roommate to put on some good music. It was Louis Armstong and the legendary song- What A Wonderful World! Immediately an idea flashed into my mind. The boy who had made the whole school tensed had a liking for music! I was exhilarated and thanked God for showing me a way. Probably this is how God acts and intervenes in our life. That night I downloaded a few English songs and copied them in my pen drive.

The next morning, soon after breakfast I called the boy into my office. He walked steadily and surprisingly wished me 'Good Morning Sir'! I offered him a chair and as he sat down with eyes full of wonder, I revealed the secret from my pocket. It was only a pen drive with 6 old hymns. He looked happy and wanted to know what the pen drive contained so precious. I told him that last night I had put some good songs for him. He looked more surprised and gently left my office. Parents came from Kolkata to take a class 11 boy from the hostel. I was sure that the boy had gone. I do not believe in destiny, but somehow I had a feeling in the deep of my heart that one day or the other I would meet him. But chances were remote. After having passed many months, I thought of writing to him. One afternoon I had finally finished writing a letter of a considerable length and had it posted.

Life doesn't remain static in the schools, students join and will leave. New faces will replace the old and varieties of emotions will carry you to another realm of fancy and delight. In between I had travelled a few more places and had the opportunity to preach the Good News to a few more people. I haven't heard of him since, but I am pretty convinced that he is no more the one he was. Hope one day I will meet him, surely he will take time to recognize me but what I wish is to see him happily settled.

We live in hope don't we?

3

The Cana Experience
Regarding Praying for Intercession

A young boy, probably a college pass out and aspiring to join a university once asked me whether Mary, the mother of God can really intercede for us or not? I was not in a mood to disappoint him, so I decided to stay away from answering his question. The boy was much disappointed and further added why the Catholic Church believed in praying to Mary for intercession? The boy was a devout Catholic and he was rational too. A week or two later, when I met him again in a park, he looked marginally happier.

Seven winters have passed with the length of seven summers and seven monsoons. And I have realized the difference between truth and fiction, life and death, *summumbonum* and *infimummalum* and most importantly; between the Words of God and the words of Politics. The biggest truth that I have learnt is that, nothing good is possible unless the Holy Spirit guides us and we are in a position to empty ourselves to God and His plans for us. With my human capacity if I try to teach people the false dogmas of any particular church, I may end up in utter frustration. But if it is the work of the Holy Spirit, no earthly power can stop me. The fundamental question not against any particular faith, but against distorting the truth and wrongly interpreting the gospel. Let us examine carefully what had happened in the wedding ceremony at Cana and how Mary, the mother of Jesus had persuaded the Son of Man to perform his first miracle.

(I would like to clarify one thing before I go any further. That is, I too love Mary and respect her as much she deserves.

The Gospel according to St. John, Chapter 2, Verse 1 to 11 reads:

> On the third day there was a wedding at Cana in Galilee, and the mother of Jesus was there. 2 Jesus also was invited to the wedding with his disciples. 3 When the wine ran out, the mother of Jesus said to him, "They have no wine." 4 And Jesus said to her, "Woman, what does this have to do with me? My hour has not yet come." 5 His mother said to the servants, "Do whatever he tells you."

> 6 Now there were six stone water jars there for the Jewish rites of purification, each holding twenty or thirty gallons.[a] 7 Jesus said to the servants, "Fill the jars with water." And they filled them up to the brim. 8 And he said to them, "Now draw some out and take it to the master of the feast." So they took it. 9 When the master of the feast tasted the water now become wine, and did not know where it came from (though the servants who had drawn the water knew), the master of the feast called the bridegroom 10 and said to him, "Everyone serves the good wine first, and when people have drunk freely, then the poor wine. But you have kept the good wine until now." 11 This, the first of his signs, Jesus did at Cana in Galilee, and manifested his glory. And his disciples believed in him.

> (English Standard Version)

The King James Version of St. John 2: 1-11 reads:

> And the third day there was a marriage in Cana of Galilee; and the mother of Jesus was there:

> 2 And both Jesus was called, and his disciples, to the marriage.

³ And when they wanted wine, the mother of Jesus saith unto him, They have no wine.

⁴ Jesus saith unto her, Woman, what have I to do with thee? mine hour is not yet come.

⁵ His mother saith unto the servants, Whatsoever he saith unto you, do it.

⁶ And there were set there six waterpots of stone, after the manner of the purifying of the Jews, containing two or three firkins apiece.

⁷ Jesus saith unto them, Fill the waterpots with water. And they filled them up to the brim.

⁸ And he saith unto them, Draw out now, and bear unto the governor of the feast. And they bare it.

⁹ When the ruler of the feast had tasted the water that was made wine, and knew not whence it was: (but the servants which drew the water knew;) the governor of the feast called the bridegroom,

¹⁰ And saith unto him, Every man at the beginning doth set forth good wine; and when men have well drunk, then that which is worse: but thou hast kept the good wine until now.

¹¹ This beginning of miracles did Jesus in Cana of Galilee, and manifested forth his glory; and his disciples believed on him.

I have quoted two most authentic versions of the Holy Bible and in both the versions we see that it is Mary, the mother of Jesus is the one to inform Jesus that the host had no more wine to serve. We can take it as a form of intercession as she had interceded on behalf of the host to her son who is the Son of God!(Mary knew it full well who Jesus was)

So what was the result?

Woman, what does this have to do with me? My hour has not yet come.

Or

Woman, what have I to do with thee? mine hour is not yet come.

So the gesture was 'negative' as we notice the two sentences that Jesus had uttered, the first one was **wh-interrogative** and the second one was **negative**. So, none of the sentences are **affirmative**. Now let us check what are the definitions of wh-interrogative, negative and affirmative sentences

Wh-Interrogative Sentence: Wh-interrogatives sentences begin with a wh-word and call for an open-ended answer. A yes or no answer isn't appropriate for these questions, nor does the question provide alternative answers. The answer can be a simple response or complex explanation.

Now let us analyse Jesus' response to his mother's request. Firstly, it was a simple response. Secondly, Jesus continued his response to another negative sentence where he says; *"mine hour is not yet come."*

It is explicit that Jesus was not willing and the tone was rejection. If not, then why did he dissuade his mother from bothering? Why he did not immediately respond to his mother and did what was needed? Jesus was neither whimsical nor disobedient. He was a devout Jew and was a strict follower of the laws. He had no intention to humiliate his mother.

What happened next?

His mother said to the servants, Do whatever he tells you./ His mother saith unto the servants, whatsoever he saith unto you, do it.

Now it is very interesting to note that Mary no more ventures to make any further request. Rather, she connects the people directly to Jesus. "Do whatever he tells you." And what was the result? We all know that water was turned into wine. Scarcity was changed into bounty, hopelessness into hope and assurance, darkness into light and despair into joy and happiness.

So what shall we assume? Did her intersession work? Mary, as the mother of Jesus is a wonderful example of submitting to the will of God, to make oneself an instrument through which God works, but whether she can intercede or not is a matter of faith and belief.

The world will be a beautiful place when every mother will be like Mary, and every father like Joseph. But Mary and Joseph are also waiting for their resurrection and judgment. They should not be insulted by being made into images and lifeless statues. Let us praise Mary as according to the scripture, not beyond that. We can say "Hail Mary, full of Grace/The lord is with you,/blessed are you among women/and blessed is the fruit of your womb Jesus."

Beware of the commandments of men…

But in vain they do worship me, teaching for doctrines the commandments of men. Matthew 15:9

(It is good if one knows Greek to read the New Testament, many of the confusions regarding the modern translations can be clarified. However, I have used the most authentic translations to avoid unnecessary controversies. I have read the chapters in Greek before attempting to write this reflection.)

4

My Ministry with the Lepers

The concept of 'youth' has been highly commercialized and distorted. What comes to our mind when we think of youth? Certain products and some stereotype dress code mostly seen in colleges and universities, in multiplexes or in shopping malls. This idea is polarized and in a way misleading. In my years of 'soul searching' I have seen the youth of this country with tattered shirts, torn vests, worn out slippers and either in decaying 'sarees' or in trousers mostly discoloured. Most of them are destitute and others dejected and rejected. Why? Because they carry their cross in the form of a disease called leprosy. How frightening is the word 'leprosy'! Let us go back to the days of Jesus. Those fearful, disfigured white appearances, living sequestered in the outskirt of the city or village. Even today people have similar notion and they do not mind even throwing their parents out of their home, if any of them contact leprosy.

However, thanks to the wisdom which God has given to us, and to those scientists who have discovered the vaccines for the cure of leprosy. It is no longer dangerous and it does not contaminate the person who stays in close proximity with lepers.

Several hospitals and hospices have been set up all over the world for lepers. The only problem is with the mindset of some people. Still many believe that leprosy is terminal and it is morally right to boycott the one suffering from it. I have had strange experiences as to the feelings and emotions of those people who have spent decades in leprosarium without contact with anyone from his/her family. Imagine, one lonely man/woman with one lonely bed...and that's all.

Badal was the leader of the group. I don't think he had any visible sign of regret for being a leper. He was vocal and always with a smile. Each time we used to meet he always greeted me with his usual smiling face:

"Jai Jesu brother, how are you" was his usual way to greet me. 'Jai Jesu' is a local expression among the Catholics to greet their brothers and sisters in Christ. I must confess that in the beginning I hesitated to shake hands with him. He had lost most of his figures to leprosy and although his wounds had dried up, the marks reminded me of the fresh wounds which I used to dress every morning. He was in his late thirties and was fond of playing cards. He had his group in his ward and playing cards was their favourite (perhaps only) time pass. I had nothing to offer to Badal, he hardly needed any counseling or spiritual guidance. What spiritual healing could you offer to a person who was always smiling, and looked happy despite having lost almost everything to leprosy? I did not get this answer even from my superior at that time. I must admit that Badal was an exceptional character.

After having spent many months I found myself standing at the same threshold from where I had started. Probably I was in need of a deeper spirituality which was provided to me by a phenomenal Canadian Jesuit, the legendary Joseph Brennan SJ.

It was my association with this hospice which became the most significant episode of my life. I have seen people suffering, have heard untold stories of the destitute and have realized God's plan for me. As a young preacher, I have felt that the world is in constant need of love and charity, and especially the youth can be instrumental in preaching the Gospel.

5

Remembering Rev. Noel S. Sen

I still remember that Sunday. It was early autumn, still Kolkata was warm and the famous St. Paul's Cathedral was all set to welcome the faithful to celebrate the Lord's Supper. The communion was over and all the participants were leaving in peace. Near the gate was the Vicar, gently shaking hands with everyone present and occasionally sharing words of greetings. I waited for everyone to leave the hall to grab a good opportunity to introduce myself. At last my turn came and he was kind enough to give me a decent hearing. I was given an appointment the following Tuesday at 9 a.m.

'Rev. Noel S. Sen, Presbyter-in-Charge' were the words written on the name plate and I was seated beside the lady, who was his secretary, waiting for my turn to come. I did not know that what I was responding to was God's calling. My first meeting with Rev. Sen had changed everything, though it took me years to realize this.

Many years later I was surprised to see him at Calcutta School of Music one evening attending a programme of a celebrated classical guitarist. Later, in 2001, when I was studying Masters in English at Calcutta University, I was elated finding him at St. Paul's Cathedral after the Eucharist.

However, I proved myself considerably ungrateful and selfish when I had learned that Rev. Noel Sen had passed away. Amidst my busy schedule I had almost forgotten my mentor, when in fact, his words of wisdom encouragement and kindness had helped me articulate my calling.

"When lilacs last in the dooryard bloom'd,

And the great star early droop'd in the western sky in the night,

I mourn'd, and yet shall mourn with ever-returning spring.

Ever-returning spring, trinity sure to me you bring,

Lilac blooming perennial and drooping star in the west,

And thought of him I love."

Walt Whitman.

Part – 2
A Spiritual Journey

*(I will extol thee, O LORD; for thou hast lifted me up,
and hast not made my foes to rejoice over me.)*

The Devil is ceaselessly trying to confuse us with several things which apparently seem important but in the eyes of God they have no value. Gold and silver are valuable to enjoy comforts of this world, but God knows what will sustain us for a good life. In this connection, one may recall what the beggar at the gate of the Temple asked from Peter and John. To him gold and silver were important for he was poor. But when he could walk on his own, he started jumping with joy. Thus, we must know what we need and only through a fellowship with God can we know this secret.

Therefore, when the sun sets and the sounds are favourably still, we can sit and examine our conscience; check the intentions of our heart and thereby correct ourselves in order to prepare for an everlasting fellowship with God.

This part of the book provides you with a few prayers, meditations, and reflections, followed by appropriate hymns. At the end you have a few more pages helping you to examine your conscience for a better understanding of the Great Mystery. I have deliberately avoided meticulous and tiresome spiritual exercises as the purpose of this book is to help you in your prayer life and not to tax you with unnecessary and insignificant rituals.

It is a very simple understanding that Jesus died on the cross to save us and we call him Lord and God. Amen! We are sinners and if we really deserve anything from God, then it is punishment. But God is kind and forgiving; His mercy is unfathomable.

Therefore, search your soul and completely surrender yourself to God. There is no cross, big or small, which the Lord doesn't share with us. Just it is Amazing Grace which saves us!

Alleluia!

6

Consolation and Desolation

The feelings stirred up by good and evil spirits are called 'consolation' and 'desolation'. This is experienced almost every day by each one of us. It is very important to a follower of Christ to know the source of our various feelings and contradictory emotion.

In order to know what God wants, we need to identify which motion of the mind comes from the good spirit and which is from the bad.

However the key question is: **where is the movement coming from and where is it leading us to?**

Spiritual consolation does not always mean happiness. In order to know what God wants, we need to identify which motion of the mind comes from the good spirit and which is from the bad. For example, a frustrated person, who has recently suffered the trauma of losing someone very dear, wants to put an end to his/her life by committing suicide. He/she is convinced that God wants him/her to die because he/she has no further hope to live on. This person neither wants to listen to counsellors nor to friends. He/she has meditated and finally, as he/she thinks, God has spoken into his/her ears and has suggested killing himself/herself. (Can God make such suggestions?)

Such crises happen to many people; we too go through such tormented situations. It may not be as tragicas death but at times we literally become HOPELESS. And at such moments, we are unable to take the right decision. During these difficult times what seem wrong may be the most appropriate thing to do.

However if any thought or feeling, which appears to be right at that moment, leads us to disappointment and makes us sad, we need to ponder on it. Remember, happiness is momentary, even a thief becomes happy after stealing some valuable things. But in the long run that happiness vanishes and guilty conscious does not allow rest in peace. It haunts.

Whereas, the happiness which lingers and leads to consolation, is a spiritual gift. This feeling, at the initial stage may be deceptive as well. The very idea of seeing a dentist is not a happy one. But after the painful feeling leaves and the swelling of the gums subsides; a great relief is experienced. How quickly we forget the excruciating pain which we had endured for over a week or a month.

Similar is our experience with God. And God being our father certainly does not like us to suffer. But there are moments when suffering is the only cure. Sometimes an experience of sadness is a moment of intimacy with God. We must remember that times of our sufferings can be moments of grace.

In the same way, happiness can deceive us. It can be illusory if such happiness results in creating doubts and uncertainties into our mind. For example, after getting up in the morning you may feel lethargic to go to work. You may decide to call up your boss and tell him/her that you are down with high fever. Immediately you are granted leave and your heart leaps up with joy! A whole day is given to you. You can relax, visit your relatives, watch television etc.

But at the end of the day when you stand before the mirror, you will certainly not like your reflection on it. Somewhere deep inside your heart a thorn will continuously prick. You will feel sorry for the lie you had told to your boss just for getting a holiday. Was it necessary? Finally, after enjoying the whole day you will go to bed with guilty conscious.

You have not only deceived your boss, but you have finally deceived yourself.

Happiness—Temporaray—-It Withers—Even A Thief Feels Happy After Stealing—But In The Due Course The Inner Conscience Haunts And Utter Frustration Prevails.

Joy-If Happiness Lingers It Turns Into Joy-It Leads Us To A Higher Spiritual Realisation-Consolation.

7

Is God in Hell?

(From Martin Luther's *Lectures on Jonah*)

And Jonah was in the belly of the fish three days and three nights.

Jonah 1:17

What a great miracle! It is beyond our comprehension how a man can survive three days and three nights inside the belly of a fish, that too in the midst of the sea. There was no light, no food...

We have no scope to refute this story as a fairy tale because it is in the Scripture. And thus God has proved here that He is omnipresent. He holds death and everything in His almighty hand and that it is an easy matter for Him to help us even in indescribable and desperate situations. He is present everywhere, in death, in hell, in the midst of our foes, yes, also in their hearts. For He has created all things, and He also governs them. This story is recorded for our sake, and God's omnipotence is here displayed so forcefully to induce us to trust and to believe Him, whether we find ourselves in the grasp of death or in the hands of our enemies. (Martin Luther, "Lectures on Jonah," Luther's Works, Vol. 19 [Saint Louis: Concordia Publishing House, 1974], p.68).

The question of "divine substance" in the soul came up once at Luther's dinner table. Luther said: "God is not bound to a locality. He cannot be excluded from any place nor can he be limited to or locked in any place. ... He is in even the lowliest creature, in a leaf or a blade of grass, yet God is nowhere." Since there were apparently some professional theologians present, the question arose whether God is everywhere potentialiter or substantialiter [in power or in substance], as a question of whether God was a potential or an essential ground. Luther: "I answer: in both ways in each creature. The creature acts by virtue of its qualitas, its qualities, but God acts...essentialiter, from the depth of his essence." The recorder of the chronicle continues: "When someone said: 'That I don't understand,' he answered: 'Don't you believe that God is at the same time present on the cross and in the virgin Mary's womb? In either case it is impossible for our reason to believe. In the same way that God can be lodged in the virgin's womb, he can also live in every creature.' Another person said: 'Would God consequently be in the devil?' 'Yes, certainly in substance even in hell...as Psalm 139[:8a] says: "If I make my bed in Sheol, thou are there".'" (Bengt R. Hoffman, Theology of the Heart [Minneapolis: Kirk House Publishers, 1998], p.84. The "Table Talk" quotations are from WT 1; 101, 27-37.)

8

Examination of Conscience

An **examination of conscience** is the act of looking prayerfully into our hearts to ask how we have hurt our relationships with God and other people through our thoughts, words, and actions. We reflect on the Ten Commandments and only on the teachings of Jesus Christ. The questions below help us in our examination of conscience. It is a half an hour meditation and preferably before supper one can sit quietly in a private chamber for this. The following steps can be helpful in examining our conscious. It is recommended to examine our conscience at least once a week.

STEP 1: Recall that you are in the presence of God.

STEP 2: Spend a moment looking over your day with gratitude for this day's gift.

STEP 3: Ask God to send you his holy spirit to help you look at your actions, attitudes and motives with honesty and patience.

STEP 4: Now review your day/week.

Recall the events of your day; explore the context of your action.

1. Do I turn to God often during the day, especially when I am tempted?

2. Do I participate at the Lord's Supper with attention and devotion on Sundays? Do I pray often and read the Bible?

3. Do I use God's name and the names of Jesus with love and reverence?

4. My Relationships With Family, Friends, and Neighbors

5. Have I set a bad example through my words or actions? Do I treat others fairly? Do I spread stories that hurt other people?

6. Am I loving of those in my family? Am I respectful of my neighbors, my friends, and those in authority?

7. Do I show respect for my body and for the bodies of others? Do I keep away from forms of entertainment that do not respect God's gift of sexuality?

8. Have I taken or damaged anything that did not belong to me? Have I cheated, copied homework, or lied?

9. Do I quarrel with others just so I can get my own way? Do I insult others to try to make them think they are less than I am? Do I hold grudges and try to hurt people who I think inferior?

STEP 6: Search for the internal movements of your heart, and your interaction with what was before you.

STEP 7: Test yourself to see whether you are living in faith, examine yourselves. Perhaps you yourselves do not realize that Christ Jesus is in you.

> "Test yourselves to see if you are in the faith; examine yourselves!
> Or do you not recognize this about yourselves, that Jesus Christ
> is in you— unless indeed you fail the test?" (2 Corinth 13:5)

READ: Paul's 2nd letter to the Corinthians.

REFLECT: What does Paul mean by "examine yourselves"?

PRAY: Pray for the wisdom to recognize Jesus Christ in you.

LISTEN: What does Jesus tell you this night as you are alone with your Lord.

ACT: During this week read about the life of any noted Christian thinker, eg. Martin Luther, John Calvin, John Wesley etc. and reflect on hoe God led him/her in God's path.

9

From the Freedom of Grace to the Shackles of the Church

Commandments of Men/Women vs Commandments of God

"But in vain they do worship me, teaching for doctrines the commandments of men."

Matt. 15:9

The purpose of this discourse chapter is to reflect and not to criticize. As Christians we are not supposed to judge others but we must act as an angel to every follower of Christ. There is no harm in pointing out the false practices and believes prevalent among many Christians. I have come across people of 'simple faith', highly misled by doctrines of humans. It is not practical to blame these people who have tremendous love for Jesus. But love is not enough, we need to work accordingly. Work should flow from our faith and hence we are justified. "To the law and to the testimony; if they speak not according to this word, it is because there is no light in them." (Isaiah 8:20)

Issue 1

Taking long and rigorous instructions before baptism and keeping a believer waiting for the next baptism session.

Scriptural references

The 'Bible' knows nothing of "instruction classes," "three-month trial periods," "getting ready" or any such waiting or delay. God's command is "now"

On the day of Pentecost, the three thousand who repented from their sins "were baptized...that day".

The Apostle Paul was immediately baptized by the first Christian disciple who came to him (Acts 9:17,18)

Issue 2

Prolonged fasting, strictly observing Mosaic laws, self-mortification etc.

Scriptural references

"But now, after that ye have known God, how turn ye again to the weak and beggarly elements, whereunto ye desire again to be in bondage?" (Galatians 4:9,10,11)

The Mosaic law declares that the whole world is a prison of sin, therefore to substitute observance of the Mosaic law for complete reliance on Christ is just the same as returning to pagan worship.

Martin Luther cautioned against fasting "with a view to meriting something by it as by a good work" arguing that certain doctrines gave believers the false idea that fasting could cancel out sin and win points towards salvation.

Issue 3

Traditions (contradictory to the Scripture) of the Church and conventions are as important as the Scripture.

Scriptural references

"But in vain they do worship me, teaching for doctrines the commandments of men." (Matt 15:9)

"For by grace are ye saved through faith; and that not of yourselves; it is the gift of God. Not of works, lest any man should boast." (Ephesians 2:8,9)

The Scripture refers to justification by faith as the gateway to scriptural holiness-

Deut 30:6; Ps 130:8; Ezek 36:25, 29; Matt 5: 48; 22:37; Luke 1:69; John 17:20-23; Rom 8:3,4; II Cor 7: 1; Eph 3: 14; 5:25-27; I Thes 5:23; Titus 2:11-14; I John 3:8; 4:17.

John Wesley observed that the living core of the Christian faith was revealed in scripture, illumined by tradition, vivified in personal experience, and confirmed by reason.

The Formative Four some:

1. Scripture

2. Tradition

3. Experience

4. Reason

N.B: Martin Luther had appealed Pope Leo X to a General Council to settle the Indulgence controversy. In 1545 Pope Paul III convened a council to meet at Trent. It met on three separate occasions. The understanding of the Gospel (by Faith alone) was rejected by Rome. In its place was substituted a Gospel that was provided by the Church alone, mediated by the sacraments alone and based on the authority of an enlarged Canon: Scripture and Tradition. They lost the Gospel of Grace!

They made the individual dependent on the church for knowledge and receiving of the Gospel.

Therefore, my dear brothers and sisters, let us not reflect on the past. The entire system is an evolution and we must look forward. It is pointless to blame any particular denomination for this mishap. No man is perfect, even the leaders of the churches have faults and they too have had their error of judgments. We often hear Pope Francis confessing the faults of the past. Even Pope John Paul II had made a list of public confessions where he apologized for the faults of the past.

Now it is time to follow the words of God and what is more important, to follow Jesus in person and in spirit. We must not forget that we all are sinners and as all the saints have a past, similarly we, sinners as we may be, have a future. We are hundred percent saints and hundred percent sinners.

Every Believer in Christ is a Priest, and is Commissioned so You and I

A re you surprised? If 'yes', then be prepared for other spiritual surprises too. And if 'no' then be sure that your understanding of the Holy Bible is perfect and such understandings are only possible if guided by the Holy Spirit. However, if you are a believer then you are a priest too. Let us read what Apostle Peter wrote in his first letter.

> You also, as living stones, are being built up a spiritual house, a holy priesthood, to offer up spiritual sacrifices acceptable to God through Jesus Christ ... But you are a chosen generation, a royal priesthood, a holy nation, His own special people, that you may proclaim the praises of Him who called you out of darkness into His marvelous light (1 Peter 2:5-9).

Now we will go back to the Old Testament and find out the reasons for God's appointment of the priests The Old Testament priests had a purpose to serve. They were chosen by God. The purpose was to serve God with their lives by offering sacrifices. The priesthood served as a picture of the coming ministry of Jesus Christ. The sacrifice of Jesus on the cross made this purpose complete.

What happened in the temple when Jesus was crucified?

The thick temple veil that covered the doorway to the Holy of Holies was torn in two by God at the time of Christ's death. (Matthew 27:51)

What was the indication?

The indication is very clear. God was indicating that the Old Testament priesthood was no more necessary. Now people could come directly to God through the great High priest Jesus Christ.

> Therefore, since we have a great high priest who has ascended into heaven, Jesus the Son of God, let us hold firmly to the faith we profess. For we do not have a high priest who is unable to empathize with our weaknesses, but we have one who has been tempted in every way, just as we are—yet he did not sin. Let us then approach God's throne of grace with confidence, so that we may receive mercy and find grace to help us in our time of need. (Hebrews 4:14-16)

And there is no other mediator between God and man as existed in the Old Testament priesthood.

> For there is one God and one mediator between God and humankind, the man Christ Jesus, who gave himself as a ransom for all people. (1 Timothy 2:5, 6)

REFLECT: Who is Jesus for me? Do I really need a priest to confess? Why I need a priest to absolve me on behalf of Jesus? God has given me wisdom and also His words. Should I follow the words of God or some practices which have no scriptural value?

READ: The first letter of the apostle Peter and Paul's first letter to Timothy.

PRAY: Let us pray for the outpouring of the Holy Spirit so that we come to look at Jesus as the High priest and repent for our hurtful ways of being.

TODAY IS THE DAY OF SALVATION

Consequently, just as one trespass resulted in condemnation for all people, so also one righteous act resulted in justification and life for all people. For just as through the disobedience of the one man the many were made sinners, so also through the obedience of the one man the many will be made righteous. (Rom 5:18, 19)

Does it mean that we all are saved?

No, unless we come personally to Christ. We must keep in mind that a gift is not a gift until it has been accepted. Paul has clearly mentioned in Romans 5:17 that we must personally receive God's "gracious" gift of life in Christ Jesus. The gift does no good if it is not received. The offer has to be accepted. Everlasting life will be enjoyed by those who have received Lord Jesus as the savior.

A beautiful hymn comes to my mind

"Nothing in my hand I bring,

Simply to Thy cross I cling;

Naked, come to Thee for dress;

Helpless, look to Thee for grace;

Foul, I to the fountain fly;

Wash me, Saviour, or I die!

While I draw this fleeting breath,

When mine eyes shall close in death,

When I soar to worlds unknown,

See Thee on Thy judgement throne,

Rock of Ages, cleft for me,

Let me hide myself in Thee."

We are neither saved by our good works, nor by our sins. Andrew Murray put it in this way: "Every human being should put all of their sins in one pile, and all of their good works in another. Then they should flee from them both to Jesus."

Jesus came on his own, but many did not receive him. But those who have received him have the right to be called 'children of God'.

A Salvation Prayer

"Dear Lord Jesus, I receive You as my Lord and Saviour. I open the door of my heart to You, and ask You to come in and live in me. I believe in my heart that God raised You from the dead. I am sorry for my sins and truly repent. By Your help and by Your Spirit, I will seek to live a life which is pleasing to You. AMEN."

"If you believe in your heart that God raised Jesus from the dead, and if you say with your mouth that Jesus is Lord, then you will be saved". (Rom 10:9)

(While you pray for your salvation or you confess to Lord Jesus, remember, you are having a personal relationship with your Lord. Do not bring anyone in between. Jesus is the Way, the Truth and the Life!)

So when are you planning for your salvation?

Is it TODAY?

Then just sit down in peace for a while and ask yourself these following questions...

a) Am I willing to be saved?

b) Am I ready to accept the gift of Salvation?

c) Do I believe that Jesus was raised from the dead by God?

If all the answers are 'YES' then go ahead, dance and sing in praise of the Lord. You are saved.

Adapted from: 'The Three parts of the Church' by Dr. Robert Frost and Ralph Mahoney.

A Few Time-honored Hymns

ON A HILL FAR AWAY

On a hill far away stood an old rugged cross,
The emblem of suff'ring and shame;
And I love that old cross where the Dearest and Best
For a world of lost sinners was slain.

So I'll cherish the old rugged cross,
Till my trophies at last I lay down;
I will cling to the old rugged cross,
And exchange it someday for a crown.

Oh, that old rugged cross, so despised by the world,
Has a wondrous attraction for me;
For the dear Lamb of God left His glory above
To bear it to dark Calvary.

In that old rugged cross, stained with blood so divine,
A wondrous beauty I see,
For 'twas on that old cross Jesus suffered and died,
To pardon and sanctify me.

To the old rugged cross I will ever be true;
Its shame and reproach gladly bear;
Then He'll call me someday to my home far away,
Where His glory forever I'll share.

George Bennard

I SAW THE LIGHT

I wandered so aimless life filed with sin
I wouldn't let my dear savior in
Then Jesus came like a stranger in the night
Praise the Lord I saw the light

I saw the light, I saw the light
No more darkness, no more night
Now I'm so happy no sorrow in sight
Praise the Lord I saw the light

Just like a blind man I wandered along
Worries and fears I claimed for my own
Then like the blind man that God gave back his sight
Praise the Lord I saw the light

I saw the light, I saw the light
No more darkness, no more night
Now I'm so happy no sorrow in sight
Praise the Lord I saw the light

I was a fool to wander and stray
Straight is the gate and narrow's the way
Now I have traded the wrong for the right
Praise the Lord I saw the light

I saw the light, I saw the light
No more darkness, no more night

Now I'm so happy no sorrow in sight
Praise the Lord I saw the light

WILL THE CIRCLE BE UNBROKEN

I was standing by my window
On one cold and cloudy day
When I saw that hearse come rolling
For to carry my mother away

Will the circle be unbroken
By and by, Lord, by and by
There's a better home a-waiting
In the sky, Lord, in the sky

I said to that undertaker
Undertaker please drive slow
For this lady you are carrying
Lord, I hate to see her go

Will the circle be unbroken
By and by, Lord, by and by
There's a better home a-waiting
In the sky, Lord, in the sky

Oh, I followed close behind her
Tried to hold up and be brave
But I could not hide my sorrow
When they laid her in the grave

Will the circle be unbroken
By and by, Lord, by and by
There's a better home a-waiting
In the sky, Lord, in the sky

I went back home, my home was lonesome
Missed my mother, she was gone
All of my brothers, sisters crying
What a home so sad and lone

Will the circle be unbroken
By and by, Lord, by and by
There's a better home a-waiting
In the sky, Lord, in the sky

We sang the songs of childhood
Hymns of faith that made us strong
Ones that mother Maybelle taught us
Hear the angels sing along

Will the circle be unbroken
By and by, Lord, by and by
There's a better home a-waiting
In the sky, Lord, in the sky

Will the circle be unbroken
By and by, Lord, by and by
There's a better home a-waiting
In the sky, Lord, in the sky

AMAZING GRACE

Amazing grace! How sweet the sound
That saved a wretch like me!
I once was lost, but now am found;
Was blind, but now I see.

'Twas grace that taught my heart to fear,
And grace my fears relieved;

How precious did that grace appear
The hour I first believed.

Through many dangers, toils and snares,
I have already come;
'Tis grace hath brought me safe thus far,
And grace will lead me home.

The Lord has promised good to me,
His Word my hope secures;
He will my Shield and Portion be,
As long as life endures.

Yea, when this flesh and heart shall fail,
And mortal life shall cease,
I shall possess, within the veil,
A life of joy and peace.

The earth shall soon dissolve like snow,
The sun forbear to shine;
But God, who called me here below,
Will be forever mine.

When we've been there ten thousand years,
Bright shining as the sun,
We've no less days to sing God's praise
Than when we'd first begun.

John Newton

I SURRENDER ALL

All to Jesus I surrender,
All to Him I freely give;
I will ever love and trust Him,
In His presence daily live.

I surrender all,
I surrender all.
All to Thee, my blessed Savior,
I surrender all.

All to Jesus I surrender,
Humbly at His feet I bow,
Worldly pleasures all forsaken;
Take me, Jesus, take me now.

All to Jesus I surrender,
Make me, Savior, wholly Thine;
Let me feel Thy Holy Spirit,
Truly know that Thou art mine.

All to Jesus I surrender,
Lord, I give myself to Thee;
Fill me with Thy love and power,
Let Thy blessing fall on me.

All to Jesus I surrender,
Now I feel the sacred flame.
Oh, the joy of full salvation!
Glory, glory to His name!

GENTLE AS SILENCE

Oh, the love of my Lord is the essence
Of all that I love here on earth.
All the beauty I see, He has given to me,
And his giving is gentle as silence.

Every day, every hour, every moment,
Have been blessed by the strength of His love.
At the turn of each tide, He is there at my side,
And his touch is as gentle as silence.

There've been times when I've turned from his presence,
And I've walked other paths, other ways,
But I've called on his name, in the dark of my shame
And his mercy was gentle as silence.

OH THE WORD OF MY LORD

(Jeremiah 1
Song For A Young Prophet)

> *O the word of my Lord*
> *Deep within my being,*
> *Oh the word of my Lord,*
> *You have filled my mind.*

Before I formed you in the womb
I knew you through and through,
I chose you to be mine.
Before you left your mother's side
I called to you, my child, to be my sign.

I know that you are very young,
But I will make you strong
I'll fill you with my word;
And you will travel through the land,
Fulfilling my command
Which you have heard.

ABIDE WITH ME

> Abide with me; fast falls the eventide;
> The darkness deepens; Lord, with me abide;
> When other helpers fail and comforts flee,
> Help of the helpless, oh, abide with me.
>
> Swift to its close ebbs out life's little day;
> Earth's joys grow dim, its glories pass away;

Change and decay in all around I see—
O Thou who changest not, abide with me.

I need Thy presence every passing hour;
What but Thy grace can foil the tempter's pow'r?
Who, like Thyself, my guide and stay can be?
Through cloud and sunshine, Lord, abide with me.

I fear no foe, with Thee at hand to bless;
Ills have no weight, and tears no bitterness;
Where is death's sting? Where, grave, thy victory?
I triumph still, if Thou abide with me.

Hold Thou Thy cross before my closing eyes;
Shine through the gloom and point me to the skies;
Heav'n's morning breaks, and earth's vain shadows flee;
In life, in death, O Lord, abide with me.

Henry F. Lyte, 1847
(Luke 24:29)

LEAD KINDLY LIGHT

Lead, kindly light, amid the encircling gloom,
lead thou me on.
The night is dark, and I am far from home;
lead thou me on.
Keep thou my feet; I do not ask to see
the distant scene, one step enough for me.
I was not ever thus, nor prayed that thou
shouldst lead me on.
I loved to choose and see my path, but now
lead thou me on.
I loved the garish day, and, spite of fears,
pride ruled my will: remember not past years.
So long thy power hath blest me, sure it still
will lead me on,

o'er moor and fen, o'er crag and torrent, till
the night is gone;
and with the morn those angel faces smile,
which I have loved long since, and lost awhile.

John Henry Newman

GUIDE ME THOU

Guide me, O thou great Redeemer,
pilgrim though this barren land;
I am weak, but thou art mighty;
hold me with thy powerful hand;
Bread of heaven,
feed me now and evermore.

Open now the crystal fountain,
whence the healing stream doth flow;
let the fiery cloudy pillar
lead me all my journey through;
strong Deliverer,
be thou still my Strength and Shield.

When I tread the verge of Jordan,
bid my anxious fears subside;
bear me through the swelling current,
land me safe on Canaan's side;
songs of praises,
I will ever give to thee.

William Williams, 1745

NEARER MY GOD TO THEE

Nearer, my God, to thee,
Nearer to thee!

E'en though it be a cross
That raiseth me.
Still all my song shall be

Nearer, my God, to thee,
Nearer, my God, to thee,
Nearer to thee!

Though like the wanderer,
The sun gone down,
Darkness be over me,
My rest a stone,
Yet in my dreams I'd be

There let the way appear,
Steps unto heav'n;
All that thou sendest me,
In mercy giv'n;
Angels to beckon me.

Then with my waking thoughts
Bright with thy praise,
Out of my stony griefs
Bethel I'll raise;
So by my woes to be.

Or if, on joyful wing
Cleaving the sky,
Sun, moon, and stars forgot,
Upward I fly,
Still all my song shall be.

Sarah F. Adams
(Psalm 42:2; Genesis 28:11-13)

WHAT A FRIEND WE HAVE IN JESUS

What a friend we have in Jesus,
All our sins and griefs to bear!
What a privilege to carry
Everything to God in prayer!
Oh, what peace we often forfeit,
Oh, what needless pain we bear,
All because we do not carry
Everything to God in prayer!

Have we trials and temptations?
Is there trouble anywhere?
We should never be discouraged—
Take it to the Lord in prayer.
Can we find a friend so faithful,
Who will all our sorrows share?
Jesus knows our every weakness;
Take it to the Lord in prayer.

Are we weak and heavy-laden,
Cumbered with a load of care?
Precious Savior, still our refuge—
Take it to the Lord in prayer.
Do thy friends despise, forsake thee?
Take it to the Lord in prayer!
In His arms He'll take and shield thee,
Thou wilt find a solace there.

Blessed Savior, Thou hast promised
Thou wilt all our burdens bear;
May we ever, Lord, be bringing
All to Thee in earnest prayer.
Soon in glory bright, unclouded,
There will be no need for prayer—

Rapture, praise, and endless worship
Will be our sweet portion there.

Joseph M. Scriven
(Exodus 33:11; John 15:13; 16:23-24)

ONE DAY AT A TIME

I'm only human, I'm just a man/woman
Help me believe in what I could be
And all that I am
Show me the stairway I have to climb
Lord for my sake, help me to take
One day at a time.

One day at a time sweet Jesus
That's all I'm askin' of you
Just give me the strength
To do every day what I have to do
Yesterday's gone sweet Jesus
And tomorrow may never be mine
Lord, help me today, show me the way
One day at a time

Do you remember when you walked among men
Well Jesus you know
If you're lookin' below, it's worse now than then
Pushin' and shovin' and crowdin' my mind
So for my sake, teach me to take
One day at a time.

One day at a time sweet Jesus
That's all I'm askin' of you
Just give me the strength
To do every day what I have to do
Yesterday's gone sweet Jesus

And tomorrow may never be mine
Lord, help me today, show me the way
One day at a time

ALTERNATE 2nd VERSE

Do you remember, when you walked among men
Well Jesus you know if you're looking below
It's worse now, than then
Cheating and stealing, violence and crime
So for my sake, teach me to take
One day at a time.

LORD I COME TO YOU

Lord I come to you
Let my heart be changed renewed
Flowing from the grace that
I have found in you
And lord I have come to know
The weakness I see in me
Will be stripped away
By the power of your love.

Hold me close let your love surround me
Bring me near draw me to your side
And as I wait
I'll rise up like an eagle
And I will soar with you
Your spirit leads me on
By the power of your love.

Lord unveil my eyes
Let me see you face to face
The knowledge of your love
As you live in me

Lord renew my mind
As your will unfolds in my life
In living everyday
By the power of your love.

SHOWERS OF BLESSING

There shall be showers of blessing:
This is the promise of love;
There shall be seasons refreshing,
Sent from the Savior above.

Showers of blessing,
Showers of blessing we need:
Mercy-drops round us are falling,
But for the showers we plead.

There shall be showers of blessing,
Precious reviving again;
Over the hills and the valleys,
Sound of abundance of rain.

There shall be showers of blessing;
Send them upon us, O Lord;
Grant to us now a refreshing,
Come, and now honor Thy Word.

There shall be showers of blessing:
Oh, that today they might fall,
Now as to God we're confessing,
Now as on Jesus we call!

There shall be showers of blessing,
If we but trust and obey;
There shall be seasons refreshing,
If we let God have His way.

Daniel W. Whittle
(Ezekiel 34:26; Psalm 115:12; Genesis 32:26)

BEYOND THE SUNSET

Beyond the sunset,
O blissful morning,
When with our Saviour
Heav'n is begun.
Earth's toiling ended,
O glorious dawning;
Beyond the sunset
When day is done.

Beyond the sunset,
No clouds will gather,
No storms will threaten,
No fears annoy;
O day of gladness,
O day unending,
Beyond the sunset,
Eternal Joy.

Beyond the sunset,
A hand will guide me
To God, the Father,
Whom I adore;
His glorious presence,
His words of welcome,
Will be my portion
On that fair shore.

Beyond the sunset,
O glad reunion,
With our dear loved ones
Who've gone before;
In that fair homeland
We'll know no parting,
Beyond the sunset
For evermore!

Virgil P Brock

LOW IN THE GRAVE HE LAY

Low in the grave he lay, Jesus my Savior,
waiting the coming day, Jesus my Lord!

Up from the grave he arose;
with a mighty triumph o'er his foes;
he arose a victor from the dark domain,
and he lives forever, with his saints to reign.
He arose! He arose! Hallelujah! Christ arose!

Vainly they watch his bed, Jesus my Savior,
vainly they seal the dead, Jesus my Lord! [Refrain]
Death cannot keep its prey, Jesus my Savior;
he tore the bars away, Jesus my Lord! [Refrain]
United Methodist Hymnal, 1989

Robert Lowry

O GOD DO THOU SUSTAIN ME

(An anabaptist hymn of prayer for strength and protection,
written by Leonhart Sommer, who died in prison, December
1573, because of his belief. Song taken from the Christian
Hymnary.)

O God, do Thou sustain me,
In grief and sore duress
Pride counter which disdains Thee
And comfort my distress.
O Lord let me find mercy
In bonds and prison bed
Men would seek to devour me
With guile and controversy
Save me from danger dread!

Thou wilt never forsake me
This firmly I believe
Thy blood Thou hast shed freely
And with it washed me.
Therein my trust is resting
In Christ, God's only Son
On him I am now building
In tribulation trusting
God will me not disown!

To die and to be living
Until my end I see
To Thee my trust I'm giving
Thou wilt my helper be
Soul, body, child companion
Herewith commit I Thee
Come soon, Lord, come and take me
From ruthless men do save me
Be honour ever to Thee.
Amen.

SWEET HOUR OF PRAYER

Sweet hour of prayer! sweet hour of prayer!
That calls me from a world of care,
And bids me at my Father's throne

Make all my wants and wishes known.
In seasons of distress and grief,
My soul has often found relief,
And oft escaped the tempter's snare,
By thy return, sweet hour of prayer!

Sweet hour of prayer! sweet hour of prayer!
The joys I feel, the bliss I share,
Of those whose anxious spirits burn
With strong desires for thy return!
With such I hasten to the place
Where God my Savior shows His face,
And gladly take my station there,
And wait for thee, sweet hour of prayer!

Sweet hour of prayer! sweet hour of prayer!
Thy wings shall my petition bear
To Him whose truth and faithfulness
Engage the waiting soul to bless.
And since He bids me seek His face,
Believe His Wrd and trust His grace,
I'll cast on Him my every care,
And wait for thee, sweet hour of prayer!

Sweet hour of prayer! sweet hour of prayer!
May I thy consolation share,
Till, from Mount Pisgah's lofty height,
I view my home and take my flight.
This robe of flesh I'll drop, and rise
To seize the everlasting prize,
And shout, while passing through the air,
"Farewell, farewell, sweet hour of prayer!"

William W. Walford
(1 Thessalonians 5:17; Revelation 8:4)

Is there any Easy Way to Resist the Feelings Stirred up by the Evil Spirit?

With the Lord nothing is difficult.

Just a month is needed. Can we give a month to our Lord?

If 'yes' then very good. We can do it. All we need is an hour each evening, the Holy Bible and a will to follow in the footsteps of the Lord. I would recommend a King James's Version of the Bible or any modern translation. Nowadays one can download the KJV application on mobile phone.

Is that all? Don't we need a guide or a retreat director?

It is good to have one, but in our day to day life seldom we get time to take a leave for a week or a fortnight to go for a retreat. Besides, arranging a retreat is also expensive. We need to book a retreat centre in advance, then a retreat director, cost of food for so many days, etc.

So, I have planned a work-out which can be tried by any one above the age of 18. One need not wait for a guide. In the course of this journey the Holy Spirit will guide us. What more we need? Our Father in heaven will send the Holy Spirit to be at our side and Lord Jesus will be our strength. Amen!

I have just made an attempt to modify the spiritual exercises practiced by various congregations and retreat directors. So that, anyone interested in soul searching can give a retreat to himself or if necessary, to family members or friends. All we need to do is to follow the instructions given below.

So let us begin.

FIRST WEEK

Sunday	Meditate upon the incidents when you have sinned by hurting your family members.	Read Psalm 31 and reflect on it. Keep a note in your personal diary about your feelings.
Monday	Lied to someone who loves you dearly.	Psalm 52
Tuesday	Deliberately disobeyed God's commands.	Psalm 25
Wednesday	Committed adultery.	Psalm 103
Thursday	Stolen (may be in the remote past by stealing some money from your dad or mom's purse, when you were a child).	Psalm 25

Friday	Denied rights to your servants, employees, workers etc.	Psalm 58
Saturday	Ask forgiveness to everyone by uttering their names distinctly. **e.g. I am sorry Bob for** .... **Please forgive me.** It is advisable to perform this phantasy exercise alone in a room.	

Eg 1. (When you ask forgiveness from someone)

Name.................I Am Sorry For Being Angry With You In 2005. I Know It Was A Wrong Decision To Have You Thrown Out Of The Job. I Am Sorry. Please Forgive Me.

Eg 2. (When you forgive someone)

Name.................... I Was Angry With You Because You Made A False Promise For Which I Had To Suffer. I Was Cursing You All These Days. Now I Forgive You. (Repeat This For A Few Times, You Will Feel Relaxed And You Will Experience The Love Of God Instantly.)

- Confess Your Sins Directly To Our Lord And Saviour Jesus Christ.

- Once Your Confession Is Over, You May Approach A Pastor Or A Spiritual Guide For Counselling.

- Remember, Once You Confess Your Sins To God With A Contrite Heart, You Are Forgiven And God Does Not Remember Our Sins.

SECOND WEEK

The meditations and prayers of the second week teach us how to follow Christ as his disciples. We reflect on Scripture passages: Christ's birth and baptism, his sermon on the mount, his ministry of healing and teaching. We are brought to decisions to change our lives to do Christ's work in the world and to love him more intimately.

Sunday	The birth of Christ.	
Monday	The baptism of Christ.	
Tuesday	The temptation of Christ.	
Wednesday	Sermon on the Mount.	
Thursday	Parables of the Good Samaritan and the Prodigal son.	
Friday	Jesus calls his first disciples.	John 1:39
Saturday	The great commission.	Matt 28:16-20

THIRD WEEK

In the third week let us meditate on Christ's Last Supper, passion, and death. We see his suffering and the gift of the Eucharist as the ultimate expression of God's love.

Sunday	The Last Supper.
Monday	Agony in the garden.
Tuesday	Christ before Pilate
Wednesday	Christ handed over to the Jews.
Thursday	Jesus' journey towards Calvary.
Friday	The Crucifixion.
Saturday	Jesus dies on the cross.

FOURTH WEEK

In this week we will meditate on Jesus' resurrection and his apparitions to his disciples. We walk with the risen Christ and set out to love and serve him in concrete ways in our lives in the world.

Sunday	The resurrection.	
Monday	The first appearance of the Lord.	
Tuesday	Acts 1:6-26	The Ascension of Jesus.
Wednesday	Acts 2: 1-13	The Pentecost.
Thursday	Acts 2: 14-36	Peter's address to the crowd.
Friday	Acts 2: 37-47	The First Converts and Life among the believers.
Saturday	Acts 3: 1-10	Peter heals a Crippled Beggar

As you have successfully completed this one month retreat, you are in a position to understand what your difficulties in walking with our Lord are. So, it has become relatively easier to remove those hindrances. You can consult your spiritual guide or a church elder to help you in overcoming the difficulties: in case you need. Otherwise, you can do it all by yourself. If you know where the problem lies, you can easily solve it. Be wise and be ready to carry your cross.

So how was the journey? Are you too tired?

I am sure now you are feeling much more relaxed and confident. You are happy because within a month you have gone so close to the Lord.

So keep it up.

FOR QUICK REFERENCE...

Psalm 31

In thee, O LORD, do I put my trust; let me never be ashamed: deliver me in thy righteousness.

2 Bow down thine ear to me; deliver me speedily: be thou my strong rock, for an house of defence to save me.

3 For thou art my rock and my fortress; therefore for thy name's sake lead me, and guide me.

4 Pull me out of the net that they have laid privily for me: for thou art my strength.

5 Into thine hand I commit my spirit: thou hast redeemed me, O LORD God of truth.

6 I have hated them that regard lying vanities: but I trust in the LORD.

7 I will be glad and rejoice in thy mercy: for thou hast considered my trouble; thou hast known my soul in adversities;

8 And hast not shut me up into the hand of the enemy: thou hast set my feet in a large room.

⁹ Have mercy upon me, O LORD, for I am in trouble: mine eye is consumed with grief, yea, my soul and my belly.

¹⁰ For my life is spent with grief, and my years with sighing: my strength faileth because of mine iniquity, and my bones are consumed.

¹¹ I was a reproach among all mine enemies, but especially among my neighbours, and a fear to mine acquaintance: they that did see me without fled from me.

¹² I am forgotten as a dead man out of mind: I am like a broken vessel.

¹³ For I have heard the slander of many: fear was on every side: while they took counsel together against me, they devised to take away my life.

¹⁴ But I trusted in thee, O LORD: I said, Thou art my God.

¹⁵ My times are in thy hand: deliver me from the hand of mine enemies, and from them that persecute me.

¹⁶ Make thy face to shine upon thy servant: save me for thy mercies' sake.

¹⁷ Let me not be ashamed, O LORD; for I have called upon thee: let the wicked be ashamed, and let them be silent in the grave.

¹⁸ Let the lying lips be put to silence; which speak grievous things proudly and contemptuously against the righteous.

¹⁹ Oh how great is thy goodness, which thou hast laid up for them that fear thee; which thou hast wrought for them that trust in thee before the sons of men!

²⁰ Thou shalt hide them in the secret of thy presence from the pride of man: thou shalt keep them secretly in a pavilion from the strife of tongues.

²¹ Blessed be the LORD: for he hath shewed me his marvellous kindness in a strong city.

²² For I said in my haste, I am cut off from before thine eyes: nevertheless thou heardest the voice of my supplications when I cried unto thee.

[23] O love the LORD, all ye his saints: for the LORD preserveth the faithful, and plentifully rewardeth the proud doer.

[24] Be of good courage, and he shall strengthen your heart, all ye that hope in the LORD.

Psalm 52

Why boastest thou thyself in mischief, O mighty man? the goodness of God endureth continually.

[2] The tongue deviseth mischiefs; like a sharp razor, working deceitfully.

[3] Thou lovest evil more than good; and lying rather than to speak righteousness. Selah.

[4] Thou lovest all devouring words, O thou deceitful tongue.

[5] God shall likewise destroy thee forever, he shall take thee away, and pluck thee out of thy dwelling place, and root thee out of the land of the living. Selah.

[6] The righteous also shall see, and fear, and shall laugh at him:

[7] Lo, this is the man that made not God his strength; but trusted in the abundance of his riches, and strengthened himself in his wickedness.

[8] But I am like a green olive tree in the house of God: I trust in the mercy of God forever and ever.

[9] I will praise thee forever, because thou hast done it: and I will wait on thy name; for it is good before thy saints.

Psalm 25

Unto thee, O LORD, do I lift up my soul.

[2] O my God, I trust in thee: let me not be ashamed, let not mine enemies triumph over me.

[3] Yea, let none that wait on thee be ashamed: let them be ashamed which transgress without cause.

[4] Shew me thy ways, O LORD; teach me thy paths.

⁵ Lead me in thy truth, and teach me: for thou art the God of my salvation; on thee do I wait all the day.

⁶ Remember, O LORD, thy tender mercies and thy lovingkindnesses; for they have been ever of old.

⁷ Remember not the sins of my youth, nor my transgressions: according to thy mercy remember thou me for thy goodness' sake, O LORD.

⁸ Good and upright is the LORD: therefore will he teach sinners in the way.

⁹ The meek will he guide in judgment: and the meek will he teach his way.

¹⁰ All the paths of the LORD are mercy and truth unto such as keep his covenant and his testimonies.

¹¹ For thy name's sake, O LORD, pardon mine iniquity; for it is great.

¹² What man is he that feareth the LORD? him shall he teach in the way that he shall choose.

¹³ His soul shall dwell at ease; and his seed shall inherit the earth.

¹⁴ The secret of the LORD is with them that fear him; and he will shew them his covenant.

¹⁵ Mine eyes are ever toward the LORD; for he shall pluck my feet out of the net.

¹⁶ Turn thee unto me, and have mercy upon me; for I am desolate and afflicted.

¹⁷ The troubles of my heart are enlarged: O bring thou me out of my distresses.

¹⁸ Look upon mine affliction and my pain; and forgive all my sins.

¹⁹ Consider mine enemies; for they are many; and they hate me with cruel hatred.

²⁰ O keep my soul, and deliver me: let me not be ashamed; for I put my trust in thee.

²¹ Let integrity and uprightness preserve me; for I wait on thee.

²² Redeem Israel, O God, out of all his troubles.

Psalm 103

Bless the LORD, O my soul: and all that is within me, bless his holy name.

2 Bless the LORD, O my soul, and forget not all his benefits:

3 Who forgiveth all thine iniquities; who healeth all thy diseases;

4 Who redeemeth thy life from destruction; who crowneth thee with lovingkindness and tender mercies;

5 Who satisfieth thy mouth with good things; so that thy youth is renewed like the eagle's.

6 The LORD executeth righteousness and judgment for all that are oppressed.

7 He made known his ways unto Moses, his acts unto the children of Israel.

8 The LORD is merciful and gracious, slow to anger, and plenteous in mercy.

9 He will not always chide: neither will he keep his anger forever.

10 He hath not dealt with us after our sins; nor rewarded us according to our iniquities.

11 For as the heaven is high above the earth, so great is his mercy toward them that fear him.

12 As far as the east is from the west, so far hath he removed our transgressions from us.

13 Like as a father pitieth his children, so the LORD pitieth them that fear him.

14 For heknoweth our frame; he remembereth that we are dust.

15 As for man, his days are as grass: as a flower of the field, so he flourisheth.

16 For the wind passeth over it, and it is gone; and the place thereof shall know it no more.

17 But the mercy of the LORD is from everlasting to everlasting upon them that fear him, and his righteousness unto children's children;

¹⁸ To such as keep his covenant, and to those that remember his commandments to do them.

¹⁹ The LORD hath prepared his throne in the heavens; and his kingdom ruleth over all.

²⁰ Bless the LORD, ye his angels, that excel in strength, that do his commandments, hearkening unto the voice of his word.

²¹ Bless ye the LORD, all ye his hosts; ye ministers of his, that do his pleasure.

²² Bless the LORD, all his works in all places of his dominion: bless the LORD, O my soul.

Psalm 58

Do ye indeed speak righteousness, O congregation? do ye judge uprightly, O ye sons of men?

² Yea, in heart ye work wickedness; ye weigh the violence of your hands in the earth.

³ The wicked are estranged from the womb: they go astray as soon as they be born, speaking lies.

⁴ Their poison is like the poison of a serpent: they are like the deaf adder that stoppeth her ear;

⁵ Which will not hearken to the voice of charmers, charming never so wisely.

⁶ Break their teeth, O God, in their mouth: break out the great teeth of the young lions, O LORD.

⁷ Let them melt away as waters which run continually: when he bendeth his bow to shoot his arrows, let them be as cut in pieces.

⁸ As a snail which melteth, let every one of them pass away: like the untimely birth of a woman, that they may not see the sun.

⁹ Before your pots can feel the thorns, he shall take them away as with a whirlwind, both living, and in his wrath.

¹⁰ The righteous shall rejoice when he seeth the vengeance: he shall wash his feet in the blood of the wicked.

11 So that a man shall say, Verily there is a reward for the righteous: verily he is a God that judgeth in the earth.

THE BIRTH OF JESUS

Matt 1:18-25 (Luke 2:1-7), Matt 2:1-12

18 Now the birth of Jesus Christ was on this wise: When as his mother Mary was espoused to Joseph, before they came together, she was found with child of the Holy Ghost.

19 Then Joseph her husband, being a just man, and not willing to make her a public example, was minded to put her away privily.

20 But while he thought on these things, behold, the angel of the LORD appeared unto him in a dream, saying, Joseph, thou son of David, fear not to take unto thee Mary thy wife: for that which is conceived in her is of the Holy Ghost.

21 And she shall bring forth a son, and thou shalt call his name JESUS: for he shall save his people from their sins.

22 Now all this was done, that it might be fulfilled which was spoken of the Lord by the prophet, saying,

23 Behold, a virgin shall be with child, and shall bring forth a son, and they shall call his name Emmanuel, which being interpreted is, God with us.

24 Then Joseph being raised from sleep did as the angel of the Lord had bidden him, and took unto him his wife:

25 And knew her not till she had brought forth her firstborn son: and he called his name JESUS.

2 Now when Jesus was born in Bethlehem of Judaea in the days of Herod the king, behold, there came wise men from the east to Jerusalem,

2 Saying, Where is he that is born King of the Jews? for we have seen his star in the east, and are come to worship him.

3 When Herod the king had heard these things, he was troubled, and all Jerusalem with him.

[4] And when he had gathered all the chief priests and scribes of the people together, he demanded of them where Christ should be born.

[5] And they said unto him, In Bethlehem of Judaea: for thus it is written by the prophet,

[6] And thou Bethlehem, in the land of Juda, art not the least among the princes of Juda: for out of thee shall come a Governor, that shall rule my people Israel.

[7] Then Herod, when he had privily called the wise men, enquired of them diligently what time the star appeared.

[8] And he sent them to Bethlehem, and said, Go and search diligently for the young child; and when ye have found him, bring me word again, that I may come and worship him also.

[9] When they had heard the king, they departed; and, lo, the star, which they saw in the east, went before them, till it came and stood over where the young child was.

[10] When they saw the star, they rejoiced with exceeding great joy.

[11] And when they were come into the house, they saw the young child with Mary his mother, and fell down, and worshipped him: and when they had opened their treasures, they presented unto him gifts; gold, and frankincense and myrrh.

[12] And being warned of God in a dream that they should not return to Herod, they departed into their own country another way.

The Baptism of Jesus
Matt 3: 13-17 (Mark 1:9-11, Lk 3;21-22, Jn 1;29-34)

[13] Then cometh Jesus from Galilee to Jordan unto John, to be baptized of him.

[14] But John forbad him, saying, I have need to be baptized of thee, and comest thou to me?

[15] And Jesus answering said unto him, Suffer it to be so now: for thus it becometh us to fulfil all righteousness. Then he suffered him.

¹⁶ And Jesus, when he was baptized, went up straightway out of the water: and, lo, the heavens were opened unto him, and he saw the Spirit of God descending like a dove, and lighting upon him:

¹⁷ And lo a voice from heaven, saying, This is my beloved Son, in whom I am well pleased.

The Temptation of Jesus

Matt 4:1-11(Mark 1:12-13, Luke 4:1-13)

4 Then was Jesus led up of the Spirit into the wilderness to be tempted of the devil.

² And when he had fasted forty days and forty nights, he was afterward anhungred.

³ And when the tempter came to him, he said, If thou be the Son of God, command that these stones be made bread.

⁴ But he answered and said, It is written, Man shall not live by bread alone, but by every word that proceedeth out of the mouth of God.

⁵ Then the devil taketh him up into the holy city, and setteth him on a pinnacle of the temple,

⁶ And saith unto him, If thou be the Son of God, cast thyself down: for it is written, He shall give his angels charge concerning thee: and in their hands they shall bear thee up, lest at any time thou dash thy foot against a stone.

⁷ Jesus said unto him, It is written again, Thou shalt not tempt the Lord thy God.

⁸ Again, the devil taketh him up into an exceeding high mountain, and sheweth him all the kingdoms of the world, and the glory of them;

⁹ And saith unto him, All these things will I give thee, if thou wilt fall down and worship me.

¹⁰ Then saith Jesus unto him, Get thee hence, Satan: for it is written, Thou shalt worship the Lord thy God, and him only shalt thou serve.

[11] Then the devil leaveth him, and, behold, angels came and ministered unto him.

Sermon on the Mount

Matt 5:1-16 (Luke 6;20-26)

5 And seeing the multitudes, he went up into a mountain: and when he was set, his disciples came unto him:

[2] And he opened his mouth, and taught them, saying,

[3] Blessed are the poor in spirit: for theirs is the kingdom of heaven.

[4] Blessed are they that mourn: for they shall be comforted.

[5] Blessed are the meek: for they shall inherit the earth.

[6] Blessed are they which do hunger and thirst after righteousness: for they shall be filled.

[7] Blessed are the merciful: for they shall obtain mercy.

[8] Blessed are the pure in heart: for they shall see God.

[9] Blessed are the peacemakers: for they shall be called the children of God.

[10] Blessed are they which are persecuted for righteousness' sake: for theirs is the kingdom of heaven.

[11] Blessed are ye, when men shall revile you, and persecute you, and shall say all manner of evil against you falsely, for my sake.

[12] Rejoice, and be exceeding glad: for great is your reward in heaven: for so persecuted they the prophets which were before you.

[13] Ye are the salt of the earth: but if the salt have lost his savour, wherewith shall it be salted? it is thenceforth good for nothing, but to be cast out, and to be trodden under foot of men.

[14] Ye are the light of the world. A city that is set on an hill cannot be hid.

[15] Neither do men light a candle, and put it under a bushel, but on a candlestick; and it giveth light unto all that are in the house.

[16] Let your light so shine before men, that they may see your good works, and glorify your Father which is in heaven.

The Parable of the Good Samaritan

Luke 10:25-37

25 And, behold, a certain lawyer stood up, and tempted him, saying, Master, what shall I do to inherit eternal life?

26 He said unto him, What is written in the law? How readest thou?

27 And he answering said, Thou shalt love the Lord thy God with all thy heart, and with all thy soul, and with all thy strength, and with all thy mind; and thy neighbour as thyself.

28 And he said unto him, Thou hast answered right: this do, and thou shalt live.

29 But he, willing to justify himself, said unto Jesus, And who is my neighbour?

30 And Jesus answering said, A certain man went down from Jerusalem to Jericho, and fell among thieves, which stripped him of his raiment, and wounded him, and departed, leaving him half dead.

31 And by chance there came down a certain priest that way: and when he saw him, he passed by on the other side.

32 And likewise a Levite, when he was at the place, came and looked on him, and passed by on the other side.

33 But a certain Samaritan, as he journeyed, came where he was: and when he saw him, he had compassion on him,

34 And went to him, and bound up his wounds, pouring in oil and wine, and set him on his own beast, and brought him to an inn, and took care of him.

35 And on the morrow when he departed, he took out two pence, and gave them to the host, and said unto him, Take care of him; and whatsoever thou spendest more, when I come again, I will repay thee.

36 Which now of these three, thinkest thou, was neighbour unto him that fell among the thieves?

37 And he said, He that shewed mercy on him. Then said Jesus unto him, Go, and do thou likewise.

The Parable of the Prodigal Son
(Luke 15:11-32)

[11] And he said, A certain man had two sons:

[12] And the younger of them said to his father, Father, give me the portion of goods that falleth to me. And he divided unto them his living.

[13] And not many days after the younger son gathered all together, and took his journey into a far country, and there wasted his substance with riotous living.

[14] And when he had spent all, there arose a mighty famine in that land; and he began to be in want.

[15] And he went and joined himself to a citizen of that country; and he sent him into his fields to feed swine.

[16] And he would fain have filled his belly with the husks that the swine did eat: and no man gave unto him.

[17] And when he came to himself, he said, How many hired servants of my father's have bread enough and to spare, and I perish with hunger!

[18] I will arise and go to my father, and will say unto him, Father, I have sinned against heaven, and before thee,

[19] And am no more worthy to be called thy son: make me as one of thy hired servants.

[20] And he arose, and came to his father. But when he was yet a great way off, his father saw him, and had compassion, and ran, and fell on his neck, and kissed him.

[21] And the son said unto him, Father, I have sinned against heaven, and in thy sight, and am no more worthy to be called thy son.

[22] But the father said to his servants, Bring forth the best robe, and put it on him; and put a ring on his hand, and shoes on his feet:

[23] And bring hither the fatted calf, and kill it; and let us eat, and be merry:

24 For this my son was dead, and is alive again; he was lost, and is found. And they began to be merry.

25 Now his elder son was in the field: and as he came and drew nigh to the house, he heard musick and dancing.

26 And he called one of the servants, and asked what these things meant.

27 And he said unto him, Thy brother is come; and thy father hath killed the fatted calf, because he hath received him safe and sound.

28 And he was angry, and would not go in: therefore came his father out, and intreated him.

29 And he answering said to his father, Lo, these many years do I serve thee, neither transgressed I at any time thy commandment: and yet thou never gavest me a kid, that I might make merry with my friends:

30 But as soon as this thy son was come, which hath devoured thy living with harlots, thou hast killed for him the fatted calf.

31 And he said unto him, Son, thou art ever with me, and all that I have is thine.

32 It was meet that we should make merry, and be glad: for this thy brother was dead, and is alive again; and was lost, and is found.

The First Disciples of Jesus
(John 1:35-42)

35 Again the next day after John stood, and two of his disciples;

36 And looking upon Jesus as he walked, he saith, Behold the Lamb of God!

37 And the two disciples heard him speak, and they followed Jesus.

38 Then Jesus turned, and saw them following, and saith unto them, What seek ye? They said unto him, Rabbi, (which is to say, being interpreted, Master,) where dwellest thou?

39 He saith unto them, Come and see. They came and saw where he dwelt, and abode with him that day: for it was about the tenth hour.

[40] One of the two which heard John speak, and followed him, was Andrew, Simon Peter's brother.

[41] He first findeth his own brother Simon, and saith unto him, We have found the Messias, which is, being interpreted, the Christ.

[42] And he brought him to Jesus. And when Jesus beheld him, he said, Thou art Simon the son of Jona: thou shalt be called Cephas, which is by interpretation, A stone.

The Great Commission

Matthew 28:16-20 (Mark 16:14-18, Luke 24:36-49, John 20:19-23, Acts1:6-8)

[16] Then the eleven disciples went away into Galilee, into a mountain where Jesus had appointed them.

[17] And when they saw him, they worshipped him: but some doubted.

[18] And Jesus came and spake unto them, saying, All power is given unto me in heaven and in earth.

[19] Go ye therefore, and teach all nations, baptizing them in the name of the Father, and of the Son, and of the Holy Ghost:

[20] Teaching them to observe all things whatsoever I have commanded you: and, lo, I am with you always, even unto the end of the world. Amen.

The Last Supper

Matthew 26:26-30 (Mark 14:22-26, Luke 22:14-23, 1Cor 11:23-26)

[26] And as they were eating, Jesus took bread, and blessed it, and brake it, and gave it to the disciples, and said, Take, eat; this is my body.

[27] And he took the cup, and gave thanks, and gave it to them, saying, Drink ye all of it;

[28] For this is my blood of the new testament, which is shed for many for the remission of sins.

²⁹ But I say unto you, I will not drink henceforth of this fruit of the vine, until that day when I drink it new with you in my Father's kingdom.

³⁰ And when they had sung an hymn, they went out into the mount of Olives.

Jesus Prays in Gethsemane
Matthew 26:36-46 (Mark 14:32-42, Luke 22:39-46)

³⁶ Then cometh Jesus with them unto a place called Gethsemane, and saith unto the disciples, Sit ye here, while I go and pray yonder.

³⁷ And he took with him Peter and the two sons of Zebedee, and began to be sorrowful and very heavy.

³⁸ Then saith he unto them, My soul is exceeding sorrowful, even unto death: tarry ye here, and watch with me.

³⁹ And he went a little farther, and fell on his face, and prayed, saying, O my Father, if it be possible, let this cup pass from me: nevertheless not as I will, but as thou wilt.

⁴⁰ And he cometh unto the disciples, and findeth them asleep, and saith unto Peter, What, could ye not watch with me one hour?

⁴¹ Watch and pray, that ye enter not into temptation: the spirit indeed is willing, but the flesh is weak.

⁴² He went away again the second time, and prayed, saying, O my Father, if this cup may not pass away from me, except I drink it, thy will be done.

⁴³ And he came and found them asleep again: for their eyes were heavy.

⁴⁴ And he left them, and went away again, and prayed the third time, saying the same words.

⁴⁵ Then cometh he to his disciples, and saith unto them, Sleep on now, and take your rest: behold, the hour is at hand, and the Son of man is betrayed into the hands of sinners.

⁴⁶ Rise, let us be going: behold, he is at hand that doth betray me.

Jesus brought before Pilate

Matthew 27:1-2 (Mark 15:1, Luke 23:1, John 18:28)

> **27** When the morning was come, all the chief priests and elders of the people took counsel against Jesus to put him to death:
>
> **2** And when they had bound him, they led him away, and delivered him to Pontius Pilate the governor.

Barabbas or Jesus?

Matthew27:15-23 (Mark 15:6-14, Luke 23:13-24, John 18:39-40)

> **15** Now at that feast the governor was wont to release unto the people a prisoner, whom they would.
>
> **16** And they had then a notable prisoner, called Barabbas.
>
> **17** Therefore when they were gathered together, Pilate said unto them, Whom will ye that I release unto you? Barabbas, or Jesus which is called Christ?
>
> **18** For he knew that for envy they had delivered him.
>
> **19** When he was set down on the judgment seat, his wife sent unto him, saying, Have thou nothing to do with that just man: for I have suffered many things this day in a dream because of him.
>
> **20** But the chief priests and elders persuaded the multitude that they should ask Barabbas, and destroy Jesus.
>
> **21** The governor answered and said unto them, Whether of the twain will ye that I release unto you? They said, Barabbas.
>
> **22** Pilate saith unto them, What shall I do then with Jesus which is called Christ? They all say unto him, Let him be crucified.
>
> **23** And the governor said, Why, what evil hath he done? But they cried out the more, saying, Let him be crucified.

Journey towards Calvary
John 19:17-22

¹⁷ And he bearing his cross went forth into a place called the place of a skull, which is called in the Hebrew Golgotha:

¹⁸ Where they crucified him, and two other with him, on either side one, and Jesus in the midst.

¹⁹ And Pilate wrote a title, and put it on the cross. And the writing was JESUS OF NAZARETH THE KING OF THE JEWS.

²⁰ This title then read many of the Jews: for the place where Jesus was crucified was nigh to the city: and it was written in Hebrew, and Greek, and Latin.

²¹ Then said the chief priests of the Jews to Pilate, Write not, The King of the Jews; but that he said, I am King of the Jews.

²² Pilate answered, What I have written I have written.

The Crucifixion of Jesus
John 19:23-37

²³ Then the soldiers, when they had crucified Jesus, took his garments, and made four parts, to every soldier a part; and also his coat: now the coat was without seam, woven from the top throughout.

²⁴ They said therefore among themselves, Let us not rend it, but cast lots for it, whose it shall be: that the scripture might be fulfilled, which saith, They parted my raiment among them, and for my vesture they did cast lots. These things therefore the soldiers did.

²⁵ Now there stood by the cross of Jesus his mother, and his mother's sister, Mary the wife of Cleophas, and Mary Magdalene.

²⁶ When Jesus therefore saw his mother, and the disciple standing by, whom he loved, he saith unto his mother, Woman, behold thy son!

²⁷ Then saith he to the disciple, Behold thy mother! And from that hour that disciple took her unto his own home.

²⁸ After this, Jesus knowing that all things were now accomplished, that the scripture might be fulfilled, saith, I thirst.

²⁹ Now there was set a vessel full of vinegar: and they filled a spunge with vinegar, and put it upon hyssop, and put it to his mouth.

³⁰ When Jesus therefore had received the vinegar, he said, It is finished: and he bowed his head, and gave up the ghost.

³¹ The Jews therefore, because it was the preparation, that the bodies should not remain upon the cross on the sabbath day, (for that sabbath day was an high day,) besought Pilate that their legs might be broken, and that they might be taken away.

³² Then came the soldiers, and brake the legs of the first, and of the other which was crucified with him.

³³ But when they came to Jesus, and saw that he was dead already, they brake not his legs:

³⁴ But one of the soldiers with a spear pierced his side, and forthwith came there out blood and water.

³⁵ And he that saw it bare record, and his record is true: and he knoweth that he saith true, that ye might believe.

³⁶ For these things were done, that the scripture should be fulfilled, A bone of him shall not be broken.

³⁷ And again another scripture saith, They shall look on him whom they pierced.

Jesus dies on the Cross
Matthew27:45-56

⁴⁵ Now from the sixth hour there was darkness over all the land unto the ninth hour.

⁴⁶ And about the ninth hour Jesus cried with a loud voice, saying, Eli, Eli, lama sabachthani? that is to say, My God, my God, why hast thou forsaken me?

⁴⁷ Some of them that stood there, when they heard that, said, This man calleth for Elias.

⁴⁸ And straightway one of them ran, and took a spunge, and filled it with vinegar, and put it on a reed, and gave him to drink.

⁴⁹ The rest said, Let be, let us see whether Elias will come to save him.

⁵⁰ Jesus, when he had cried again with a loud voice, yielded up the ghost.

⁵¹ And, behold, the veil of the temple was rent in twain from the top to the bottom; and the earth did quake, and the rocks rent;

⁵² And the graves were opened; and many bodies of the saints which slept arose,

⁵³ And came out of the graves after his resurrection, and went into the holy city, and appeared unto many.

⁵⁴ Now when the centurion, and they that were with him, watching Jesus, saw the earthquake, and those things that were done, they feared greatly, saying, Truly this was the Son of God.

⁵⁵ And many women were there beholding afar off, which followed Jesus from Galilee, ministering unto him:

⁵⁶ Among which was Mary Magdalene, and Mary the mother of James and Joses, and the mother of Zebedees children.

The First Appearance of the Lord. (The Resurrection of Jesus)
Luke 24:1-12 (Matthew 28:1-10, Mark 16:1-8, John 20:1-10)

24 Now upon the first day of the week, very early in the morning, they came unto the sepulchre, bringing the spices which they had prepared, and certain others with them.

² And they found the stone rolled away from the sepulchre.

³ And they entered in, and found not the body of the Lord Jesus.

⁴ And it came to pass, as they were much perplexed thereabout, behold, two men stood by them in shining garments:

⁵ And as they were afraid, and bowed down their faces to the earth, they said unto them, Why seek ye the living among the dead?

⁶ He is not here, but is risen: remember how he spake unto you when he was yet in Galilee,

⁷ Saying, The Son of man must be delivered into the hands of sinful men, and be crucified, and the third day rise again.

⁸ And they remembered his words,

⁹ And returned from the sepulchre, and told all these things unto the eleven, and to all the rest.

¹⁰ It was Mary Magdalene and Joanna, and Mary the mother of James, and other women that were with them, which told these things unto the apostles.

¹¹ And their words seemed to them as idle tales, and they believed them not.

¹² Then arose Peter, and ran unto the sepulchre; and stooping down, he beheld the linen clothes laid by themselves, and departed, wondering in himself at that which was come to pass.

The Ascension of Jesus
Acts 1:6-26

⁶ When they therefore were come together, they asked of him, saying, Lord, wilt thou at this time restore again the kingdom to Israel?

⁷ And he said unto them, It is not for you to know the times or the seasons, which the Father hath put in his own power.

⁸ But ye shall receive power, after that the Holy Ghost is come upon you: and ye shall be witnesses unto me both in Jerusalem, and in all Judaea, and in Samaria, and unto the uttermost part of the earth.

⁹ And when he had spoken these things, while they beheld, he was taken up; and a cloud received him out of their sight.

¹⁰ And while they looked stedfastly toward heaven as he went up, behold, two men stood by them in white apparel;

¹¹ Which also said, Ye men of Galilee, why stand ye gazing up into heaven? this same Jesus, which is taken up from you into heaven, shall so come in like manner as ye have seen him go into heaven.

¹² Then returned they unto Jerusalem from the mount called Olivet, which is from Jerusalem a sabbath day's journey.

¹³ And when they were come in, they went up into an upper room, where abode both Peter, and James, and John, and Andrew, Philip, and Thomas, Bartholomew, and Matthew, James the son of Alphaeus, and Simon Zelotes, and Judas the brother of James.

¹⁴ These all continued with one accord in prayer and supplication, with the women, and Mary the mother of Jesus, and with his brethren.

¹⁵ And in those days Peter stood up in the midst of the disciples, and said, (the number of names together were about an hundred and twenty,)

¹⁶ Men and brethren, this scripture must needs have been fulfilled, which the Holy Ghost by the mouth of David spake before concerning Judas, which was guide to them that took Jesus.

¹⁷ For he was numbered with us, and had obtained part of this ministry.

¹⁸ Now this man purchased a field with the reward of iniquity; and falling headlong, he burst asunder in the midst, and all his bowels gushed out.

¹⁹ And it was known unto all the dwellers at Jerusalem; insomuch as that field is called in their proper tongue, Aceldama, that is to say, The field of blood.

²⁰ For it is written in the book of Psalms, Let his habitation be desolate, and let no man dwell therein: and his bishoprick let another take.

²¹ Wherefore of these men which have companied with us all the time that the Lord Jesus went in and out among us,

²² Beginning from the baptism of John, unto that same day that he was taken up from us, must one be ordained to be a witness with us of his resurrection.

²³ And they appointed two, Joseph called Barsabas, who was surnamed Justus, and Matthias.

²⁴ And they prayed, and said, Thou, Lord, which knowest the hearts of all men, shew whether of these two thou hast chosen,

²⁵ That he may take part of this ministry and apostleship, from which Judas by transgression fell, that he might go to his own place.

²⁶ And they gave forth their lots; and the lot fell upon Matthias; and he was numbered with the eleven apostles.

The Coming of the Holy Spirit
Acts 2:1-13

2 And when the day of Pentecost was fully come, they were all with one accord in one place.

² And suddenly there came a sound from heaven as of a rushing mighty wind, and it filled all the house where they were sitting.

³ And there appeared unto them cloven tongues like as of fire, and it sat upon each of them.

⁴ And they were all filled with the Holy Ghost, and began to speak with other tongues, as the Spirit gave them utterance.

⁵ And there were dwelling at Jerusalem Jews, devout men, out of every nation under heaven.

⁶ Now when this was noised abroad, the multitude came together, and were confounded, because that every man heard them speak in his own language.

⁷ And they were all amazed and marvelled, saying one to another, Behold, are not all these which speak Galilaeans?

⁸ And how hear we every man in our own tongue, wherein we were born?

⁹ Parthians, and Medes, and Elamites, and the dwellers in Mesopotamia, and in Judaea, and Cappadocia, in Pontus, and Asia,

¹⁰ Phrygia, and Pamphylia, in Egypt, and in the parts of Libya about Cyrene, and strangers of Rome, Jews and proselytes,

¹¹ Cretes and Arabians, we do hear them speak in our tongues the wonderful works of God.

¹² And they were all amazed, and were in doubt, saying one to another, What meaneth this?

¹³ Others mocking said, These men are full of new wine.

Peter Addresses the Crowd

Acts 2:14-36

¹⁴ But Peter, standing up with the eleven, lifted up his voice, and said unto them, Ye men of Judaea, and all ye that dwell at Jerusalem, be this known unto you, and hearken to my words:

¹⁵ For these are not drunken, as ye suppose, seeing it is but the third hour of the day.

¹⁶ But this is that which was spoken by the prophet Joel;

¹⁷ And it shall come to pass in the last days, saith God, I will pour out of my Spirit upon all flesh: and your sons and your daughters shall prophesy, and your young men shall see visions, and your old men shall dream dreams:

¹⁸ And on my servants and on my handmaidens I will pour out in those days of my Spirit; and they shall prophesy:

¹⁹ And I will shew wonders in heaven above, and signs in the earth beneath; blood, and fire, and vapour of smoke:

²⁰ The sun shall be turned into darkness, and the moon into blood, before the great and notable day of the Lord come:

²¹ And it shall come to pass, that whosoever shall call on the name of the Lord shall be saved.

²² Ye men of Israel, hear these words; Jesus of Nazareth, a man approved of God among you by miracles and wonders and signs, which God did by him in the midst of you, as ye yourselves also know:

²³ Him, being delivered by the determinate counsel and foreknowledge of God, ye have taken, and by wicked hands have crucified and slain:

²⁴ Whom God hath raised up, having loosed the pains of death: because it was not possible that he should be holden of it.

²⁵ For David speaketh concerning him, I foresaw the Lord always before my face, for he is on my right hand, that I should not be moved:

²⁶ Therefore did my heart rejoice, and my tongue was glad; moreover also my flesh shall rest in hope:

²⁷ Because thou wilt not leave my soul in hell, neither wilt thou suffer thine Holy One to see corruption.

²⁸ Thou hast made known to me the ways of life; thou shalt make me full of joy with thy countenance.

²⁹ Men and brethren, let me freely speak unto you of the patriarch David, that he is both dead and buried, and his sepulchre is with us unto this day.

³⁰ Therefore being a prophet, and knowing that God had sworn with an oath to him, that of the fruit of his loins, according to the flesh, he would raise up Christ to sit on his throne;

³¹ He seeing this before spake of the resurrection of Christ, that his soul was not left in hell, neither his flesh did see corruption.

³² This Jesus hath God raised up, whereof we all are witnesses.

³³ Therefore being by the right hand of God exalted, and having received of the Father the promise of the Holy Ghost, he hath shed forth this, which ye now see and hear.

³⁴ For David is not ascended into the heavens: but he saith himself, The Lord said unto my Lord, Sit thou on my right hand,

³⁵ Until I make thy foes thy footstool.

³⁶ Therefore let all the house of Israel know assuredly, that God hath made the same Jesus, whom ye have crucified, both Lord and Christ.

The First Converts

Acts 2:37-47

³⁷ Now when they heard this, they were pricked in their heart, and said unto Peter and to the rest of the apostles, Men and brethren, what shall we do?

³⁸ Then Peter said unto them, Repent, and be baptized every one of you in the name of Jesus Christ for the remission of sins, and ye shall receive the gift of the Holy Ghost.

³⁹ For the promise is unto you, and to your children, and to all that are afar off, even as many as the LORD our God shall call.

⁴⁰ And with many other words did he testify and exhort, saying, Save yourselves from this untoward generation.

⁴¹ Then they that gladly received his word were baptized: and the same day there were added unto them about three thousand souls.

⁴² And they continued stedfastly in the apostles' doctrine and fellowship, and in breaking of bread, and in prayers.

⁴³ And fear came upon every soul: and many wonders and signs were done by the apostles.

⁴⁴ And all that believed were together, and had all things common;

⁴⁵ And sold their possessions and goods, and parted them to all men, as every man had need.

⁴⁶ And they, continuing daily with one accord in the temple, and breaking bread from house to house, did eat their meat with gladness and singleness of heart,

⁴⁷ Praising God, and having favour with all the people. And the Lord added to the church daily such as should be saved.

Peter Heals a Crippled Beggar

Acts 3:1-10

3 Now Peter and John went up together into the temple at the hour of prayer, being the ninth hour.

² And a certain man lame from his mother's womb was carried, whom they laid daily at the gate of the temple which is called Beautiful, to ask alms of them that entered into the temple;

³ Who seeing Peter and John about to go into the temple asked an alms.

⁴ And Peter, fastening his eyes upon him with John, said, Look on us.

⁵ And he gave heed unto them, expecting to receive something of them.

⁶ Then Peter said, Silver and gold have I none; but such as I have give I thee: In the name of Jesus Christ of Nazareth rise up and walk.

⁷ And he took him by the right hand, and lifted him up: and immediately his feet and ankle bones received strength.

⁸ And he leaping up stood, and walked, and entered with them into the temple, walking, and leaping, and praising God.

⁹ And all the people saw him walking and praising God:

¹⁰ And they knew that it was he which sat for alms at the Beautiful gate of the temple: and they were filled with wonder and amazement at that which had happened unto him.

The above extracts are taken from the King James Version (KJV) of the Holy Bible.

APPENDIX - 3

A Few Inspirational Quotes

1. I have held many things in my hands, and I have lost them all; but whatever I have placed in God's hands, that I still possess. - Martin Luther

2. All who call on God in true faith, earnestly from the heart, will certainly be heard, and will receive what they have asked and desired. - Martin Luther

3. Our Lord has written the promise of resurrection, not in books alone, but in every leaf in springtime. - Martin Luther

4. A dog barks when his master is attacked. I would be a coward if I saw that God's truth is attacked and yet would remain silent. - John Calvin

5. The torture of a bad conscience is the hell of a living soul. - John Calvin

6. He who allows oppression shares the crime. - Desiderius Erasmus

7. Give light, and the darkness will disappear of itself. - Desiderius Erasmus

8. The Bible shows the way to go to heaven, not the way the heavens go. - Galileo Galilei

9. I am not going to Heaven because I have preached to great crowds or read the Bible many times. I'm going to Heaven just like the thief on the cross who said in that last moment: 'Lord, remember me.' - Billy Graham

10. God has given us two hands, one to receive with and the other to give with. - Billy Graham

11. Give me one hundred preachers who fear nothing but sin, and desire nothing but God, and I care not a straw whether they be clergymen or laymen; such alone will shake the gates of hell and set up the kingdom of heaven on Earth. - John Wesley

12. You have one business on earth – to save souls. - John Wesley

Epilogue

My Lord was not crucified in between two candles and inside a beautiful cathedral. So, I do believe in preaching the Gospel amidst hostile environment and uncomfortable situations. I do not do anything of my own; it is the Holy Spirit who guides me amidst impediments and adversities.

I have seen beautiful chapels, furnished prayer halls, the best of the schools and the most modernized seminaries. Those places, due to lack of spirituality have degenerated into spiritual graveyards. I have also seen how we get involved in things other than what God wants us to do. If I have a calling and I call myself a preacher/pastor/priest etc, my priority should be to preach the words of God and to save souls.

My academic knowledge, reading of various books on theology and on the History of Religion have definitely helped me to arrange my thoughts in a structured way, but I found the real joy of discovering Christ in my humility and in my confession that Jesus is my Lord and my God.

Like Ignatius of Loyola I want to pray:"Take and receive O Lord my liberty

Take all my will my mind my memory.
Do Thou direct, and govern all and sway,
Do what Thou wilt, command and I obey.
Only Thy grace and love on me bestow
Possessing these all riches I forgo.

Only Thy grace and love on me bestow
Possessing these all riches I forgo.

All things I hold, and all I won are Thine,
Thine was the gift, to Thee I all resign
Do Thou direct, and govern all and sway,
Do what Thou wilt, command and I obey.

GOD BLESS YOU!

"I cannot and will not recant anything,
for to go against conscience
is neither right nor safe.
Here I stand, I can do no other,
so help me God. Amen."

Martin Luther

Milton Keynes UK
Ingram Content Group UK Ltd.
UKHW041612160923
428812UK00001B/77